A DANCE with the DEVIL

D1738816

MICHELLE WILLINGHAM

Published by Michelle Willingham
www.michellewillingham.com

ISBN-13: 978-0-9906345-4-6

Cover by Carrie Divine/Seductive Designs
Photo by Period Images
Interior formatting by Author E.M.S.

Published in the United States of America.

OTHER BOOKS BY MICHELLE WILLINGHAM

MacEgan Brothers Series
(Medieval Ireland)
Her Warrior Slave
"The Viking's Forbidden Love-Slave" (novella)
Her Warrior King
Her Irish Warrior
The Warrior's Touch
Taming Her Irish Warrior
"The Warrior's Forbidden Virgin" (novella)
"Voyage of an Irish Warrior" (novella)
Surrender to an Irish Warrior
"Pleasured by the Viking" (novella)
"Lionheart's Bride" (novella)
Warriors in Winter

The MacKinloch Clan Series
(Medieval Scotland)
Claimed by the Highland Warrior
Seduced by Her Highland Warrior
"Craving the Highlander's Touch" (novella)
Tempted by the Highland Warrior
"Rescued by the Highland Warrior" (novella in the
Highlanders anthology)

The Accidental Series
(Victorian England/Fictional Province of Lohenberg)
"An Accidental Seduction" (novella)
The Accidental Countess
The Accidental Princess
The Accidental Prince

Other Titles
"Innocent in the Harem"
(A novella of the sixteenth-century Ottoman Empire)
"A Wish to Build a Dream On"
(time travel novella to medieval Ireland)
"A Dance with the Devil"

CHAPTER ONE

"They say Castle Keyvnor is haunted."

"Don't be silly. There's no such thing as ghosts." Jane Hawkins considered herself to be a sensible young woman. She didn't believe in anything of the supernatural variety, and she rather thought the spirits of the dead had better things to do than frighten the living. Her friend, Lady Marjorie, was of another mind and appeared deliciously scared at the idea.

"I've heard that late at night, sometimes you can hear the ghost of Lady Banfield wailing for her lost son," Marjorie murmured. "What if we see her in the hallway?" She shuddered at the thought. "I cannot imagine anything worse."

"We're going to be fine. I imagine people exaggerate the story because it makes it more interesting." Despite her attempt to reassure Marjorie, Jane couldn't help but admit to herself that the castle was not exactly the sort described in fairy stories—no, this was a castle that would terrify small children. Tall and imposing, formed

1

from dark stone, Castle Keyvnor stood upon the edge of the sea cliff with turrets rising against the shadows. The darkening evening skies added to its somber presence.

"At least *you* don't have to live here," Marjorie muttered. "I, on the other hand, am doomed. Unless I can find a gentleman to marry who will take me away from this horrible place." She glanced over at her mother and sister, who were sleeping on opposite sides of the coach. "Why did my father have to acquire a castle like this?"

Lady Marjorie's father, Allan Hambly, had inherited the earldom of Banfield, which meant he would reside at Castle Keyvnor for some time. Several other families had traveled for the reading of the late Earl of Banfield's will, and Marjorie had insisted that Jane come with them.

Her stomach twisted in knots at the thought. She didn't belong here with all the nobility. She was a vicar's daughter, and though she and Marjorie had been friends since they were young girls, Jane knew her place.

"We're going to find a husband for you, too," Marjorie insisted. Her friend smiled brightly, but Jane didn't share her optimism. Yes, a husband would indeed help her circumstances. Her parents were aging, and Jane doubted if there was enough money to support them for very much longer. She had to either marry or find a position as a governess or a companion.

No one wants to marry a vicar's daughter, she reminded herself. She had no dowry to speak of and no title. Marjorie meant well, but Jane knew the reality of her situation. At best, she might wed a merchant or a soldier. But her chances of marrying well were not good.

"I think you have a better chance of finding a

husband," she told Marjorie. "I'm no one. At least you're an earl's daughter."

"Don't denigrate yourself," her friend insisted. "You're quite beautiful. And if there's a wealthy titled gentleman, I'm certain he'll be besotted with you."

Jane didn't argue, though she was a realist by nature. There would be no offers from titled lords—not for someone like her. She understood that, even if Marjorie didn't.

The coach slowed as it traveled down the narrow lane leading toward the coast. A light rain spattered against the window of their coach, and Jane pulled her shawl closer in anticipation of the cold. "I'll be glad to stop traveling," she told her friend. The wheels had jolted them over every rock and rut in the road until it felt as if her teeth were rattling out of her skull.

"So will I. Though I imagine my knees will still be shaking." Marjorie grimaced as she glanced back at her mother and older sister Tamsyn, once again. "I don't know how they're sleeping through this." Her other three sisters had traveled in a second coach with their father. Jane was grateful not to be crammed inside with them, or worse, having to ride with the servants.

A few minutes later, the coach came to a stop, and a footman opened the door to the coach. At that, Lady Banfield awakened, along with Tamsyn.

"Heavens, what a terrible journey," Lady Banfield moaned. "I will be glad to sleep in a bed of my own this night."

"So will I." Tamsyn yawned and stretched. She accepted help from the footman as she disembarked from the coach, followed by her mother and sister. Jane waited to be the last one out of the vehicle, being careful to keep a slight distance from the family.

It was startling to see so many other coaches also

arriving at Castle Keyvnor. Jane counted at least four others, and all around her, servants were busy unloading baggage.

"You'd best stay with the family, Miss Hawkins," the footman warned. "With so many people about, it's safer."

She nodded and trailed behind Marjorie and her mother. The afternoon light was waning as evening approached. When Jane took another step closer to them, a violent gust of wind caught at her shawl. She tried to seize the wet wool, but the gust tore it from her fingers and sent it flying toward a group of guests.

"Oh dear," she murmured, hurrying after it. It was the only shawl she owned, and in cold weather such as this, she could not afford to lose the garment.

To her horror, she saw it tumble upon the ground, the wind tossing it until it came to rest at a gentleman's feet. He was busy speaking with another man, and Jane didn't dare approach.

He might move away. If he did, then she could snatch it quickly, and no one need know. But already she could see the Banfield family walking toward the drawbridge over the dry moat. She ought to be with them, but instead, she was chasing after her errant shawl.

The gentleman's expression transformed a moment, and then he bent down, picking up the sodden, gray wool. "What have we here?"

"It looks as if that maid has lost her shawl," the other man teased.

I'm not a maid, she wanted to tell them, but didn't. She didn't truly belong here and had only come at Marjorie's insistence.

But when the first gentleman turned to face her, Jane felt her face grow red. Goodness. This man was surely an angel, fallen from Heaven. Or perhaps a devil. His blond hair was tipped with darker ends, and his green eyes were like Connemara marble. He had a strong jaw that hinted of wickedness, and his mouth was firm and held the hint of a smile. He was exactly the sort of gentleman who might steal a lady into dark corners. And worse, she would enjoy it.

"Have you lost something?" the man asked, holding out the shawl.

Jane nodded, unable to speak. The English language had fled her mouth, and if she'd tried to speak a single word, surely she would have failed.

After a moment, while the man continued to offer the shawl, she realized that she was supposed to actually reach out and take it. Good Lord, she had clearly lost her brain.

"Th—thank you," she stammered as she accepted the shawl. "My lord."

With a nod to him, she fled back toward Marjorie and the others, hurrying until she reached the drawbridge. Her cheeks were burning with embarrassment. And yet, she wondered if the man was as attractive as she'd imagined.

She knew she shouldn't look back, but could not resist the urge. The moment she turned, she saw him staring at her. Not with unkindness or with a harmful intent…but almost as if he found her to be a curiosity. Jane pulled the wet shawl across her shoulders, tightening it as if it were a shield.

And then he smiled at her, tipping his hat.

"She's not for you."

Devon Lancaster, fourth son of Viscount Newbury, glanced over at his best friend, Jack Hazelwood, Lord St. Giles. "And why not? She's beautiful."

The young lady who had lost her shawl had a heart-shaped face, framed by light brown hair and blue eyes the color of cornflowers. She was painfully shy, but Devon found himself intrigued by her.

"Because she's a servant, that's why." Jack dismissed her immediately. "She might be fair enough for a tête-à-tête, but she's not meant for marriage."

"Why would you assume that?" He hadn't seen the young lady carrying any baggage for Lord Banfield or his family. It seemed that she had hurried to catch up to one of the earl's daughters.

"Because of her clothing. Now if you're looking for a rich wife, you should look toward Banfield's daughters or Beck's relations. Anyone except Lady Cassandra, that is. Otherwise, I'll gut you." Jack offered a friendly smile, but Devon knew better than to even look toward Lady Cassandra Priske. His best friend had invited himself to Castle Keyvnor for the sole purpose of courting the lady—not because he expected to inherit anything from the late earl. He had arrived the day before, along with their mutual friends, Michael Beck, Teddy Lockwood, and Hal Mort.

As for himself, Devon had come along with his own purpose, which also had nothing to do with the will-reading—he wanted to find a wife. And though he knew what was expected of him—to woo a wealthy, respectable woman—he wouldn't mind finding someone who captivated him.

"I wouldn't dream of even looking in Lady Cassandra's direction," Devon said. "But I must admit, finding a wife is a daunting proposition. Marriage is so very…permanent." His own parents had an arranged union that was civil, but neither of them had felt any sort of affection toward one another. If anything, his mother had held a great deal of animosity toward the viscount, due to his numerous affairs.

Devon didn't want that sort of marriage. Perhaps it was a ridiculous idea, but he preferred to have affection toward his wife. He wanted someone who was a friend as well as the future mother of his children. That, at least, would make the marriage bearable. And if she happened to be beautiful with a passionate nature, he wouldn't mind that, either.

He joined Jack as they walked back toward the drawbridge. It was early evening, but the sun had not yet descended. "Has Lady Cassandra arrived?"

His friend shrugged. "Not yet, that I know of."

They crossed over the drawbridge, beneath an ancient iron portcullis. The moment he crossed into the outer bailey, Devon felt as if something icy had brushed his shoulder. He glanced at his friend, who didn't appear to notice anything. Then, the chilly sensation vanished, leaving him to wonder if he'd imagined it.

Still, he couldn't help but broach the idea. "What do you know about Castle Keyvnor?" asked. "Do you think it's true that the place has ghosts?"

"I doubt it. But Beck did point out a spot where they apparently beheaded a man." Jack pointed toward a patch of green lawn within the courtyard. "They said he was a traitor to King Henry VIII." His expression darkened. "Beck thinks this castle is cursed. I simply think it's old. Everything creaks when it's seven hundred years old."

Devon hung back a moment, motioning for Jack to do the same. The young woman whose shawl he'd rescued was standing a few paces behind the Earl of Banfield. He studied her more closely and realized that Jack was right. Her clothing was very plain—she wore a dark blue serge gown and the gray shawl he'd rescued earlier, along with a gray bonnet. Her light brown hair was bound up away from her face, and her blue eyes were downcast.

But in spite of her plain attire, he couldn't quite tear his gaze from her. There was something about her face that drew him in, making him wonder about her secrets.

What would she look like with her hair down around her shoulders, those blue eyes staring back at him with interest? Her body was thin, but there was no denying the curve of her breasts or the gentle sway of her hips.

Devon wanted to know her name—needed to know it. No, she likely wasn't a candidate for marriage. But there was no harm in getting acquainted with the lady and finding out why she was here.

"Beck invited me to play a game of billiards," Jack told him. "Do you want to come?"

Devon shook his head. "I've another challenge in mind." With a nod toward the young lady, he added, "I'll wish you luck in your game."

"One doesn't need luck when one possesses great skill. You are welcome to join us in a later game, if you enjoy losing."

"I might," Devon agreed.

Just then, he heard the sound of barking. A small black poodle raced toward the center of the courtyard, snarling at the empty air. The hair on the dog's spine stood on end, and he growled at the unseen enemy. It was the very spot where Jack claimed the traitor's beheading had taken place.

"Are you certain the dog hasn't seen a ghost?" Devon teased. Though he had never actually witnessed a specter, he hadn't imagined the icy chill that had passed over him.

"I doubt it. But dogs do sense things." At that, the animal lifted his leg and proceeded to relieve himself upon the execution site.

Devon bit back a grin. "Well, if there was a ghost there, I imagine he is quite put out."

"Or marked." Jack shook his head and started toward the castle keep. "In the meantime, I'll bid you good hunting with your mysterious servant girl."

"She's not a servant. Her speech is too refined for that." Her tone and diction were nothing at all like a servant's. And yet, he hadn't missed the way the woman held herself back from Lord Banfield's family. She appeared too young to be a governess, truthfully.

But he intended to find out exactly who she was.

Jane had never felt so overwhelmed in all her life. Castle Keyvnor was the largest estate she had ever seen. After enjoying a cup of tea and a light repast, she had walked behind Lord Banfield and his daughters, staring in bewilderment at all the rooms. The stone walls and Gothic architecture reminded her of a medieval castle, especially with the large tapestries upon the walls.

"I'll need a map," she said to Marjorie. "I'm going to get lost in this place."

"So will I," her friend agreed. "But as long as we get lost with a handsome gentleman to guide us back, it's all right by me." Marjorie leaned in closer. "Did you ever find out the name of the man who gave back your shawl?"

Jane blinked a moment. "I didn't realize you saw that."

"I notice *everything*." Marjorie smiled at her. "And once I find out who it is, I will ask Father to introduce you."

"Don't bother. If he possesses a title, he will have no interest in a vicar's daughter." She gripped the edges of her gray shawl, well aware of her plain appearance.

Every garment she owned was gray, dark blue, or brown, and modest, as befit a clergyman's daughter.

"He might," her friend offered, though Jane didn't believe it. All of a sudden, a barking noise caught her attention, and she spied a black poodle racing down the hallway.

"Oscar! Come back!" a young woman called out, hurrying toward the dog. Jane saw the animal bolt around the corner and on impulse, she decided to help.

"I'll be back," she said, as she picked up her skirts and hurried after the dog. She had three dogs of her own at home and had no doubt she could help retrieve the animal.

"You'll get lost!" Marjorie warned.

"Then I will ask for directions and find you again." Jane smiled and raced around the corner, just in time to see the poodle change directions again. He skidded to a halt in front of a stone staircase, and she slowed her pace. If she ran toward him, he would consider it a game and scamper away once again. Instead, she took slow footsteps.

"You're a mischievous fellow," she remarked to the dog. "Why did you run away?" The dog wagged its tail at her, and she suspected he was only playing.

"Do you need help, my lady?" came a male voice from behind her.

Jane turned and saw the very gentleman who had rescued her shawl. Oh dear. Of all the men to find her, why did it have to be the man who tied her tongue into knots?

"I—yes, I think so. He got away from one of the ladies, and I thought I would try to retrieve him." She tried to keep her attention squarely upon the poodle, for if she dared to look at the gentleman, she would undoubtedly lose every coherent thought.

"That's kind of you." He drew closer and added, "I suppose I should introduce myself, since there is no one here to do it properly. I am Devon Lancaster."

For a second, she'd thought he'd said Devil Lancaster. He did indeed resemble a devilish sort of man, with his dark blond hair and green eyes.

"And you are Lord of what?" she blurted out without thinking. Heavens, what was wrong with her? She wanted to knock her head against the wall. "I'm sorry. I meant only that—that is, your title—"

"I don't have one," he answered cheerfully. "I'm the fourth son of Viscount Newbury. I'm nothing but a mister." He eyed the dog and took another step toward him. "And you are?"

"Jane Hawkins," she answered. "Also Lady of nothing. I'm a friend of Lady Marjorie's."

"Any relation to the late earl?" he asked.

"None at all." She offered a sheepish smile. "I feel like an imposter, just for being here. Marjorie insisted that I come with her family, but I don't really belong."

Mr. Lancaster leaned in and murmured, "Don't tell anyone, but I shouldn't be here either. I'm friends with Lord St. Giles and Lord Michael Beck, and I joined them at their invitation."

"Then we're both imposters." Jane relaxed somewhat, for it did feel that neither one of them ought to be here. And now that she knew he was not a titled lord, she felt less conspicuous.

"So we are." He took another step toward the dog, who was sniffing at the steps and snarling. "I'm going to pick him up on the count of three. I think I can come up behind him before he notices. One…"

"I don't think he's going to let you do that." Her own dogs would delight in racing away, provoking her to chase after them.

"Two." Mr. Lancaster held up his hand in a pause. "Three." He lunged toward the poodle, who shot across the hallway in a full run.

"Blast it." He took off after the dog, and Jane joined him in a run, laughing as she did.

"I told you he wouldn't let you seize him." She gripped her skirts while her shawl slipped down her shoulders. "Dogs love to be chased. Or at least, mine do."

"What do you suggest?"

They continued running down another narrow hallway until the dog scampered halfway to the end.

"We need to corner him," Jane said, huffing as she kept up with Mr. Lancaster. "If we can trap him inside one of the rooms, that will do. And then we can find his owner."

"Good idea." He motioned for her to spread out, and they slowed their pace as they reached the end of the hallway.

"Oscar!" The young woman who owned the dog came running toward them, her dark hair falling loose from its chignon.

"Don't worry, we'll help you catch him," Mr. Lancaster reassured the woman. "Let's try to drive him toward an open room, and we can close the door."

"How about the room at the end of that hallway," Jane suggested. "You could run ahead of the dog and cut him off so he can't go down the other way."

"All right. And the two of you try to herd him inside." Mr. Lancaster moved toward the end of the hallway, racing past Oscar to block his path. As he took a step toward the animal, the poodle scampered in the opposite direction—exactly as they'd hoped.

"Perfect," Jane said. "Now let's guide him toward the doorway." She joined with the other young woman, and as they moved forward, Jane introduced herself and Mr. Lancaster.

"I am Lady Cassandra Priske," the woman answered. "Thank you so much for helping me catch up to Oscar."

"You're welcome." Jane offered a friendly smile, and when Oscar saw the pair of them approaching, he ran into the room. "Trapped," she proclaimed in triumph.

"Bless you both." Lady Cassandra hurried after him, and Jane blocked the doorway so the poodle could not run away. She thought about joining Lady Cassandra, but stopped herself when she realized there were two gentlemen already inside the billiards room.

"I think she has control of her dog once more," Mr. Lancaster said. "You did well, Miss Hawkins."

She stepped away from the billiards room, feeling her cheeks warm beneath his praise. "So did you. And now I am hopelessly lost within this castle. I don't suppose you know the way back to the drawing room?"

"I do indeed. Will you allow me to escort you there?" He offered his arm. "And if we find any escaped animals along the way, I am certain we will manage well enough."

His charming smile slipped past her defenses, making her all too aware of his masculinity. She rested her hand upon the crook of his arm, feeling her heartbeat stammer within her chest.

This isn't real, she reminded herself. *He's only being a gentleman.*

And yet, she was entirely too conscious of the way his coat clung to his broad shoulders. His green eyes gleamed with a blend of amusement and a hint of wickedness.

When they reached the drawing room, Jane felt the need to apologize. "I am sorry to have disturbed you," she said. "I imagine you never intended to spend your evening chasing after a poodle."

"No," he agreed. "But were it not for Oscar's misbehavior, I might not have met you, Miss Hawkins. And it was a pleasure, indeed."

CHAPTER TWO

"It was a mistake to bring her with us," Regina Hambly, Lady Banfield, said to her husband. She motioned for the elderly footman to bring the tea tray, and the servant obeyed, setting it down on the end table. Regina poured two cups, adding a nip of sugar to her husband's tea.

"We had no choice," the earl countered. "She was summoned."

"But it will only cause a scandal if anyone finds out who Jane really is. If they discover that she's—"

"They won't." The earl took his cup and sat across from her. "I see no reason to tell her anything. Let Jane believe she is here as Marjorie's companion. And if we are careful, we can arrange to give her whatever portion she is entitled to, without anyone ever learning the truth."

Regina steepled her fingers together and nodded toward the footman. "Bronson, leave us, if you will."

The older servant had difficulty hearing and likely hadn't heard a word of their conversation, but she didn't want to take any chances. Once he had closed the door behind him, she turned back to Allan. "We have no idea how much Jonathan Hambly left her. If it's a small amount, no one will think anything of it, and we can hide the scandal. But if he left her a fortune, everyone will want to know why."

"We will handle that once we know." Lord Banfield straightened. "For now, we will keep her identity quiet. I think it would be best."

"Sometimes I wish we had sent her away." Regina sighed. When Jane was born, they had felt sorry for the newborn child. A child born out of wedlock could never have a respectable life. It had seemed kinder to let her be raised by the vicar and his wife instead of sending her to an orphanage. At least Jane had been given a home with a loving family. Regina had thought it a perfect solution at the time, never imagining that the past would come back to threaten everything.

"We did the right thing for Jane," Allan said quietly. "I believe that."

She moved beside him and took his hand. "I am only glad that Evelyn did not live to hear about Jane. It would have broken her spirit."

Her husband squeezed her palm. "No one can know of this, Regina. Especially Jane."

"It will be our secret."

"You should come with us to breakfast, Jane," Marjorie said. "Why would you take a tray in your room? Don't you want to see Mr. Lancaster again?"

Jane mustered a smile and shook her head. "It's better if I stay here. I really don't belong with everyone else."

Marjorie frowned. "And what about me? And Tamsyn and Rose and Morgan and Gwyn? You don't think you're worthy of eating with *us*?" Her friend rolled her eyes.

"That's different. I've known you all my life." Marjorie was practically a sister to her, as were the other girls. They had played together as children and not once had the girls looked down on her, despite their family's comfortable wealth.

But her true reason for avoiding public gatherings was a sense that she didn't truly belong among the nobility. Everyone else had been summoned to receive a portion of their inheritance. Jane was merely here as a companion.

Marjorie sighed. "Jane, you must come. Otherwise, you're behaving like a long-suffering martyr."

The invisible blow was more hurtful than she'd imagined. Jane tightened her lips and admitted, "All of my clothing was handed down to me. Whenever I'm around the other ladies, I cannot help but feel their disapproval."

"Then borrow one of my gowns."

"I cannot do that, Marjorie. It would be a lie. This is who I am. I'm not trying to behave like an heiress."

Her friend rolled her eyes and opened her trunk. She rummaged around until she found a white long-sleeved muslin gown. It was very plain with only a bit of ribbon trim along the hem and cuffs. "Wear this. And if you do not, I will have Tamsyn hold you down while I dress you. You are coming with us to breakfast, or we will drag you by your hair."

Her pride burned at the thought. "There's no need for this, Marjorie."

"Good. Then you must realize that my sisters drive me into madness. I need you there as my friend so I won't murder them. You're keeping me from being arrested."

Marjorie waved her maid to come over. "Penny, help Jane into this gown." She crossed her arms and waited.

Although Jane felt like a caterpillar being pinned with butterfly wings, she held still and allowed Penny to dress her in a chemise and short stays. The gown had no buttons and the maid helped slide it over her head, pulling the laces tightly around the bodice to fit it to her. Jane sent a dismayed look toward Marjorie. "I look as if one good sneeze would cause me to pop out of this."

Her friend smiled brightly. "Well, that *would* give us an interesting discussion over breakfast, wouldn't it? Do try to keep your bosom under wraps."

Jane seized a pillow and swatted her friend while Marjorie giggled. "Careful, or you might tear a seam."

A knock came at the door, and she heard the voice of Lady Tamsyn calling out, "Are you both ready?"

"Not yet. But come in and see Jane," Marjorie answered.

Her older sister opened the door, and the moment Tamsyn spied Jane, she smiled. "You do look beautiful."

The white gown made her feel entirely too conspicuous. "I still don't think this is a good idea. It doesn't truly fit, and I—"

"Nonsense," Marjorie took her hand and half-dragged her to the door. "You're coming with us, and that is final."

Lady Tamsyn took her other hand. "I couldn't agree more."

Despite her misgivings, Jane promised herself that she would try not to speak very much and blend in as well as she could. One meal might not be so bad.

But her stomach was twisted into knots of vicious nerves. In this gown, every curve was accentuated, and she worried that the other guests would get the wrong idea about her. They might believe she was one of the ladies meant to inherit.

She followed Marjorie and Tamsyn into the dining

room and saw several other guests milling about. The room reminded her of a cathedral with its tall Gothic windows and the ribbed vaulted ceiling. Upon the wall, she saw four pointed stone arches, and a fire burned in the hearth behind the large mahogany table.

Lord and Lady Banfield greeted their daughters and nodded a welcome to Jane. She steeled herself and followed Marjorie to the sideboard where she took a plate. A short older man with graying hair stood behind her. He smiled brightly, "Good morning to you. I don't believe we've met as of yet. I am John Hunt, solicitor to the late Earl of Banfield."

Jane nodded in greeting. "Good morning." With an apologetic shrug, she said, "I'm not related to Lord Banfield. I am Jane Hawkins, a friend of Lady Marjorie's. I came as her companion." She chose a slice of toast for her plate, along with a spoonful of strawberry jam.

The solicitor blinked a moment. "Didn't Lord Banfield tell you? You were summoned along with the others. In fact, it was *most* important that you be here, Miss Hawkins."

"Let's not speak of this right now," Lord Banfield interrupted. With a sharp look toward Mr. Hunt, he stood beside Jane. "She is here, and that is all that matters." The solicitor muttered an apology and took a step back.

But Jane felt as if the floor had dropped out from beneath her. "What is Mr. Hunt talking about, Lord Banfield?"

"We will discuss this in private," the earl promised. "Not in front of all these people." Again, he glared at the solicitor. "Is that quite clear, Mr. Hunt?"

The solicitor seemed taken aback. "Do you mean to say that she doesn't know?"

"Know what?" A sense of alarm had gathered inside

her. Mr. Hunt was behaving as if she were related to the late earl.

But the new Lord Banfield stepped between them. In a low voice, he added, "One more word from you, Mr. Hunt, and I will deduct a portion of your salary."

"Well." The solicitor let out a sigh of air and added, "Don't the eggs look delicious? I believe I shall have to try some."

But Jane had lost her appetite. Her mind was reeling from the solicitor's revelation. To Marjorie, she whispered, "What was your father talking about?"

Her friend appeared just as bewildered. "I have no idea." She took Jane by the hand and brought her to the table. Leaning in, she added, "But I promise you, I will find out everything." She beamed and whispered, "Wouldn't it be wonderful if you turned out to be a secret heiress?"

Jane picked at her toast, swirling the strawberry jam in a circle around the surface. "I don't know about that."

She had always known she was adopted. The vicar and his wife had made certain she was aware of her birth circumstances. Her real mother, Emily Hawkins, had been a governess in the household of a neighboring family, before she had been seduced and left pregnant. Once she had begun to show, she had been dismissed at once from her post.

The Hambly family had felt sorry for Emily's plight and had arranged for her to stay with the vicar and his wife, John and Mary Engelmeyer. The Engelmeyers had taken Emily into their home, offering to raise the baby as their own. But the young woman had died in childbirth, and it was a miracle that Jane had survived.

We were so grateful that the good Lord blessed us with you, her adopted mother, Mary had told her. *I could*

not have children of my own, but I thank God every day
that your mother gave you into our care.

Jane had never known any other parents, save the Engelmeyers, but it hadn't mattered. They had loved her and reared her as their own. Now, it felt as if her safe life had been ripped apart. Her real father was somehow related to the Earl of Banfield, it seemed.

What if he was here now, at Castle Keyvnor? Her mind couldn't quite grasp it, and she pushed her plate away, untouched.

"Are you all right, Jane?" Marjorie asked.

"I think I need to take a walk. Some fresh air might help," she admitted. She stood from her chair and pulled her gray shawl over her shoulders.

Just as she was leaving the dining room, she nearly bumped into Mr. Lancaster. He wore a bottle green coat and buff-colored breeches. His expression turned warm, and he teased, "Are you fleeing at the sight of me, Miss Hawkins?"

Her cheeks flushed. "No, I simply thought I'd take a walk after breakfast."

"It looks as if it will rain," he pointed out. She bit her lip, feeling foolish for not even considering the weather. And when she glanced at the dining room window, she realized he was right. Dark clouds hovered in the sky and a light sprinkling of rain was spattering against the glass, sliding down in rivulets.

"Well, then, I suppose I shall simply explore the house."

"Be wary of the ghosts," he warned, with a light smile. "Beck was telling me about a screaming noise he heard from one of the turrets. Or it could have been the wind."

"I don't believe in ghosts," she said. "But thank you for the warning." She couldn't help but smile in return, and her heart fluttered at the intense warmth in his green eyes. He was staring at her with unconcealed interest.

"You look lovely this morning. The gown suits you." His deep voice warmed her, and Jane felt her blush deepen at his compliment. She wasn't accustomed to men noticing her, and she hardly knew how to respond. She almost blurted out, *It's Marjorie's,* but thought better of it and simply voiced a thank you.

"Enjoy your breakfast," she bade him. "I'll go wandering through the halls instead of outside."

Mr. Lancaster's smile faded, and he turned serious. "You'd better take an escort with you. While I don't think anyone here would harm a lady, it's never wise to go anywhere alone."

She gave a noncommittal nod. "I understand." Though truthfully, she didn't really want to be around anyone just now. Her friends were all enjoying their breakfasts, and she'd lost all appetite for food after Mr. Hunt's revelation. Right now, she wanted a moment to be alone and think about what to do.

Lord Banfield held the answers she wanted. It was clear that he'd known she was meant to be here. But why? No one had ever told her anything about her father, except that he had seduced her mother and left her. A tightness gathered in her stomach. She didn't want to meet the man, even if he *was* here. Anyone who would take advantage of a woman and then leave her behind with a pregnancy deserved absolutely nothing.

She excused herself, but before she could go, Marjorie handed her a note. "Jane, I was asked to give you this."

She took the message and opened it. Lady Banfield asked to meet with her in the kitchen in private. Jane wasn't certain why she had chosen that location, but the countess might be busy planning the menu for tonight's dinner with the cook. It was a strange note, but she saw no reason to question it.

Perhaps Lady Banfield would have the answers Jane was searching for.

Devon didn't feel right letting Miss Hawkins go off alone. Although she seemed like a quiet, composed young woman, something put his instincts on alert. She appeared upset. He tried to join the others at breakfast, conversing with everyone, but he couldn't shake the feeling that she shouldn't be exploring the house. Though she had agreed not to go alone, he had a feeling that she had done so anyway.

It wasn't as if anyone here had a reason to threaten her. Most of the men he'd met were decent fellows, half of them married. And yet, he found himself hurrying through breakfast, wanting to be certain she was all right. Several of the men were getting ready to attend the funeral of Thomas Vail in Hollybrook Park, but since Devon was not acquainted with the family, he was staying behind.

His friend, Michael Beck, leaned in. "Did you hear what the solicitor said about her?" He tilted his head toward the door.

"Miss Hawkins, you mean?"

"Yes. It appears that she stands to inherit from the late earl. It seems Jack was wrong about her being a servant. You might want to pursue her, after all."

Devon stiffened at Michael's suggestion, for it made him seem like a fortune hunter. "Miss Hawkins told me she is only here as a friend to Lady Marjorie."

There was a gleam in Beck's eye. "Then she was lying to you. Mr. Hunt was delighted to see her and made no secret of the fact that she's an heiress. Everyone here heard him."

Devon didn't quite believe that. Miss Hawkins didn't appear to be the sort of woman who would lie about an inheritance. But then, he knew very little about her, except that she was shy.

His instincts warned that she was shy enough that she would not want to trouble a servant to be her escort. It was quite possible that she might walk through a castle of this size, unaccompanied.

"I will see you later," he told Beck. Then he took a piece of buttered toast with him as he left the dining room. Devon walked down the hallway in search of Miss Hawkins, but there was no trace of her.

As he neared the main staircase, he felt an icy chill settle near his shoulders. The rest of his body was warm, and the cold sensation was unnerving. Though he knew most people didn't believe in ghosts, he left himself open to possibilities. He did believe in an afterlife, and who was he to say if ghosts did or did not exist?

He felt a bit foolish but muttered to the air around him, "If you are a ghost, you might tell me if Miss Hawkins is all right." The coldness moved to his neck, like a clammy hand formed of ice. It didn't seem at all reassuring.

"Well, then, could you tell me where she's gone?"

The icy presence seemed to leave him, and he was now feeling like a complete dolt. Talking to air? Honestly?

But when a door at the end of the hall seemed to blow open of its own accord, the hair stood up on the back of his neck. The door was light and swung easily on its hinges. Most likely it was a breeze that had blown it open. Logic told him that much, even as he walked toward it. He saw one of the footmen enter, carrying a tray, and realized that it was the doorway leading to the servants' entrance.

I am losing my wits, he thought to himself as he walked to the end of the hallway. *Miss Hawkins would not possibly go this way.*

But the icy presence settled over his shoulders once again, as if an invisible spirit were guiding him. He was stopped by an older female servant who glared at him. Her dark hair was stretched beneath a cap, and she blocked his path. "Are you lost, sir?" The portly woman rested both hands on her hips.

"No, Miss—"

"It's Mrs. Bray," she corrected. "I am the housekeeper at Castle Keyvnor. Did you need something?" The look of irritation on her face suggested that she wanted him gone from here as soon as possible.

"I was looking for Miss Hawkins. Someone said she came this way." *A ghost,* if one might be accurate about it. That is, if ghosts were real and if one had indeed led him here. He still felt foolish about it, but he was a man of intuition.

"She was here earlier, aye. But she's gone now." The housekeeper waited a moment, and then added, "Now, if you'll excuse me, sir, I have work to do."

Interesting. Out of all the possible places Miss Hawkins could have gone, the kitchen was among the least likely. But if a ghost had indeed guided him here, it must be a benevolent spirit. He turned back the way he had come, and almost instantly felt the same icy chill in the air. A few paces away, he spied the poodle, Oscar. The dog's hair stood on end, and he let out a low growl.

"It's all right," he told the dog. "If it *is* a ghost, it's a helpful one."

Oscar sniffed at the floor a moment and then trotted

back toward the kitchen. Devon felt the coldness encircle his shoulders, and he remarked, "Well, you took me this far. Now what?"

The door leading outside suddenly swung open of its own accord. With that, the coldness intensified upon his skin, and he shoved back an instinctive fear. He could not deny the presence of something otherworldly, but it was unnerving to see doors open in such a way.

And yet—the spirit had led him here to where Jane had been, only a moment ago. For that reason, he murmured, "Lead on."

Devon felt the brush of cold air sweep past him, and he followed it down the hall.

Lady Banfield wasn't in the kitchen. Jane asked Mrs. Bray if she had seen her, but no one had. How very odd. She could not understand why the countess had asked her to come and then was not here.

Jane walked down the hallway, wondering what to do now. The wooden floors gleamed, and she took a moment to study her surroundings. Upon one wall, she saw portraits of the former Earls of Banfield, going back for several hundred years. She stopped when she saw the last portrait, of Jonathan Hambly, Lord Banfield. The painting must have been created when he was a younger man, for he had a dashing smile and a hint of mischief in his eyes.

She turned away and nearly jolted when she saw another man standing before her. He had red hair and a beard with bright blue eyes. His clothing reminded her of Henry VIII, with a velvet cap and what appeared to be pantaloons. Beneath one arm, he carried a lute. Was the man an actor, hired to perform in a play?

"I beg your pardon," Jane remarked. "You startled me."

"Such was not my intent." The man nodded toward the portrait. "'Twas most tragic that Lord Banfield had no living heirs, my lady. His only son died at the age of five years."

"That is very sad," Jane agreed. She wasn't certain who the gentleman was, or why he was here, but before she could leave, he continued talking.

"His wife, Lady Banfield, went mad with grief. She tried to have another child for years and could never succeed." In a low voice, he added, "They say the turret is heavy with her grief, and you often can hear her screaming." His smile held a hint of darkness. "Do you believe in ghosts, my lady?"

In spite of herself, goosebumps rose over Jane's skin. She mustered a weak smile. "Not really. If you'll excuse me, sir, I was trying to find Lady Banfield. The living one," she amended.

"You might try the outbuilding behind the kitchen," he suggested. "I saw her near the herb garden." He tipped his velvet cap, smiling, and a few droplets of water poured down.

"Thank you." Jane excused herself and walked toward the back of the house. She had already decided that if Lady Banfield was not there, she would simply find her later. This felt rather like a merry chase, when she had no idea why the countess had even summoned her.

She pulled the door open and as she did, she spied Mr. Lancaster standing just outside in the rain. Her pulse quickened at the sight of him, and she clenched one of her gloves.

"Why, hello," she greeted him with a nod. "I didn't expect to see you here, so soon after breakfast."

He held the door open for her. "Neither did I, to be honest. But I was concerned that you might be out walking alone. Do you want me to ring for a servant to accompany you? A maid, perhaps?"

"I have no maid. Not really. Marjorie does." Jane huddled against the doorway, and the light rain dampened her hair and Marjorie's borrowed white gown. She should have thought to ask for her bonnet and an umbrella. Instead, she remained where she was, searching for a glimpse of Lady Banfield.

"If you need an escort, I could watch over you," he offered.

"I am fine, truly. You needn't worry over me." His very presence made her nervous. She was all too aware of his tall form, of his dark blond hair and the light stubble of beard on his chin. His green eyes searched hers, and she felt a sudden rush of emotion that she couldn't describe.

"You seemed very upset after breakfast," he said. "What happened?"

"It's nothing." She tried to brush off the incident, for there was no need for him to be involved. "Just a misunderstanding with the solicitor."

His gaze turned kind. "If anyone here is bothering you, Miss Hawkins, I can put a stop to it."

She gave him a sheepish smile. "Thank you for the offer, but I'm certain you have better things to do than worry about me."

His expression warmed, and her skin tightened when his attention shifted over her face as if he were memorizing her. "Not at all, Miss Hawkins." He offered his arm and admitted, "I find you fascinating. And given the choice between spending time playing billiards with friends or walking through the rain with a beautiful woman, it is no hardship at all. Wait here, and I shall return momentarily." She did and saw him speak with a footman. When he returned a few moments later, he carried an umbrella. "Shall we?"

Though her mind was urging her not to, her heart was enchanted by the idea of walking through the rain with a handsome gentleman. *Why not? It isn't as if he's going to offer for someone like me.*

Why shouldn't she take advantage of a moment like this, even knowing it would lead nowhere?

"All right," she said, placing her hand upon his arm. Mr. Lancaster opened the umbrella, and they stepped onto the brick stairs that led toward the back garden.

"Did you want to walk through the flower gardens?" he asked.

"Actually, I was supposed to meet with Lady Banfield." She almost told him about the actor she had seen, but then decided not to. "I had heard she was in one of the outbuildings behind the kitchen."

Mr. Lancaster guided her toward the garden pathway. "Then we will find her, if she is here."

The rain poured down over them, and Jane couldn't help but huddle closer to him. "I'm sorry," she said, "it's just that I'm trying not to get Marjorie's day dress wet."

He moved the umbrella to shield more of her, even though it put him in the rain. "Better?"

"No. You should remain under the umbrella. So long as it doesn't bother you that I have to stand closer."

"Not at all," he murmured.

It *did* feel nice to walk in the rain beside such a handsome gentleman. Her wayward heart couldn't help but beat faster with him so near. She could almost imagine his arm around her waist, or what it would be like to rest her head against his broad chest.

For some unknown reason, it felt as if she could trust

this man, though she couldn't say why. And right now, she wanted a friend to listen to the burden she carried.

"The solicitor said that I was supposed to be here for the will reading," she blurted out. "It bothers me, because Lord Banfield told me nothing of this. I'm an orphan, Mr. Lancaster. There is no reason for me to inherit anything."

"You could be a distant cousin," he offered. His voice was low, almost soothing. "Why should it bother you? I would think you would be glad to hear of this."

It frightens me, she almost said. But then, she didn't want to admit it to anyone. Instead, she stopped beside the herb garden. "I hadn't met Lord Banfield before he died, and my adopted parents certainly have never spoken of him."

"And what of your real parents?" he pressed. "Did they know the earl?"

His question only solidified her fears. For that was the true question, wasn't it? "I never knew them. My mother died when I was born, and I never learned who my father was. Suffice it to say, I come from a very humble family."

He studied her a moment before his face relaxed. "Miss Hawkins, it wasn't my intent to pry."

His words did soothe her, somewhat, for she believed him. "I know. But I did think you should know that I am not from a titled family, nor do I possess any wealth. I am unsuitable to be anyone's bride."

A hint of a smile tugged at his mouth. "If you were trying to talk me into marriage, it isn't working, Miss Hawkins."

It took her a second to realize he was teasing. She braved a smile and added, "Good. If I ever marry, it will be a man of my own station."

"Someone quiet and boring, no doubt." Mr. Lancaster

led her toward the outbuilding behind the kitchen, and the rain began to slow down.

"There is nothing wrong with a safe and boring man," Jane said. "At least then, I would know what to expect."

"An exciting husband would make life entirely too unpredictable." The glint in his eyes suggested he was teasing her again.

"I prefer a man who is a creature of habit."

He started to lean in closer. "You ought to try an unpredictable man before you make your decision, Miss Hawkins. You might find that you like him better."

His nearness sent a flare of heat within her, one she found startling. She caught the scent of his shaving soap, and for a moment, she imagined what it would be like to be in this man's embrace. No, a man like Devon Lancaster would never be boring. His green eyes were locked upon hers, and in them she saw his interest. Her attention was drawn to his mouth, and wild thoughts of a kiss suddenly tangled in her imagination. She backed away, only to feel the raindrops soaking through her gown.

"Am I making you uncomfortable, Miss Hawkins?"

Jane hardly knew how to answer that. "Not exactly. But I thought I should be honest with you, so you don't get the wrong idea about me. You do seem to be following me."

"My reasons are honorable, I assure you," Mr. Lancaster said. "I simply didn't want you to go off alone without an escort. Then, too, this house is haunted. One never knows if a ghost is benevolent or vindictive."

She narrowed her gaze at him. "You don't *really* believe in ghosts, do you?"

He glanced behind him and admitted, "I have felt the presence of *something* in this house. And honestly, I've witnessed quite a few strange things thus far. I prefer to remain open to possibilities."

Jane wasn't certain what to make of that. He opened the door to the outbuilding and gestured for her to enter. "After you." He accompanied her inside and put down the umbrella. The interior of the room was warm, and she smelled the comforting aroma of drying herbs. Rosemary, sage, and thyme hung in tied bundles from the ceiling. But there was no sign of Lady Banfield. The gentleman who told her he had seen the countess here must have been mistaken, for why would the countess be here in a place like this? She also wondered if the note had been false.

In the corner, she spied a stone staircase. "Where do you suppose that leads?" she wondered aloud.

Mr. Lancaster shrugged. "We can go down and see for ourselves if you like. I imagine it's the wine cellar."

Jane heard the sound of a bottle shattering down below. The noise startled her, and she wondered if someone needed help. She started to go down the stairs, but Mr. Lancaster warned, "Wait. Let me see if it's safe first." He hurried traveled down the spiral stairs, pushing open the wooden door at the bottom, and Jane followed. The interior was lit by candles set into iron sconces on the wall. Shadows flickered against the stone, and she took a step back.

Perhaps this wasn't such a good idea.

A coldness settled over her shoulders, and she pulled her shawl tight. It did nothing to diminish the chill, and she called out, "Lady Banfield?" But instinctively, she knew the countess would not answer.

Only silence reigned over the wine cellar. Jane saw a broken bottle on the far end of the room and a puddle of red wine beneath it. She moved closer and crossed the room, looking to see if anyone was nearby, but there was no one. It seemed that the bottle must have been poorly balanced on the wine rack and fell of its own accord.

"She's not here," Mr. Lancaster said. "No one is. We should go back."

Jane agreed with his suggestion wholeheartedly. But when they turned around, the wooden door slammed shut. The gust of air from the door caused the candle beside it to go out, leaving them with only one candle for light.

Mr. Lancaster rushed to the door and pulled hard, but it appeared that someone had locked them inside. He let out a low curse and pounded on the wood. "Open the door!"

But when they listened, there came only the sound of a man's laughter. Fear iced through her, and Jane was now certain someone had lured them here on purpose. Was it the actor she had met in the hallway, the one who had known so much about the family? Or was it someone else who was trying to cause a scandal by locking her in the wine cellar with Mr. Lancaster?

"Can you force it open?" she ventured.

His response was to lunge at the door, smashing his shoulder against the wood. He let out a hiss of pain and rubbed at his arm. "Apparently not. Why would anyone do something like this?"

"I don't know."

But their question was answered a moment later when a voice muttered. "Leave Castle Keyvnor, Jane Hawkins. You are not wanted here."

Mr. Lancaster pounded on the door again, demanding to be let out. But they both heard the retreating sound of footsteps going up the stairs. For the next several minutes, he called out for help, beating against the wine cellar door. But no one came.

He paused a moment to catch his breath and asked,

"What was that all about? Who would threaten you?"

"I truly don't know." But she was beginning to think that there was more to her inheritance than she'd guessed. Was the gentleman Lord Banfield's nephew, the heir apparent? Or did her captor somehow believe that she was meant to gain a fortune from the late Lord Banfield? There were no answers at all.

Her teeth chattered from the frigid air all around them, and she shivered. Her gown was sodden from the raindrops, and she couldn't seem to get warm. Mr. Lancaster continued pounding on the door, shouting out for help. But it seemed that no one heard him.

A moment later, he removed his coat and drew it over her shoulders. "I am sorry this happened, Miss Hawkins."

"It wasn't your fault." She clung to his coat, and the warmth of his body lingered within the wool. "Thank you for lending me this."

In the dim light, his face had grown somber. "Someone is trying to harm you. But I can't think why."

Jane shook her head. "I've no idea. I wasn't even supposed to be here. Or at least…that's what I thought."

She had honestly believed that Marjorie had brought her along as a companion. Despite her initial misgivings, her friend had convinced her that it would be an exciting journey and a chance to meet new people. Now, she was beginning to wonder if Marjorie had known anything about this, or whether it had been her father's suggestion.

"Do you think someone believes you are taking his or her inheritance?" Mr. Lancaster prompted.

"I highly doubt it. Even if I am mentioned in his will, it can't be more than a pittance. I'm not even related to Lord Banfield." She shrugged, drawing the edges of his coat closer. "But you may be right. Perhaps someone is afraid."

"Your father may have been related to the earl," he said. "You may find out who he was."

All her life she had imagined stories, but in the end, she didn't truly want to know. "It doesn't matter. He left us behind and never looked back."

She leaned back against the wall, only to step away when she found it frigid. "How are we going to get out of here, Mr. Lancaster?"

"I can try to pick the lock. Or if we hear voices, we can pound on the door until someone lets us out."

Her teeth began chattering, and she said, "At least there's little chance of us dying down here. The only problem is the scandal."

"There won't be one," he reassured her. "When we hear someone approaching, I will hide myself behind the shelves of wine. You will go on without me. Keep the door unlatched, and I'll wait until you are gone before I leave."

It relieved her to hear of it. "Thank you for that. I doubt that either one of us would want to be forced into marriage."

"You're a beautiful woman, Miss Hawkins, and I would not find it a hardship. But the truth is, I am the fourth son of a viscount. I have nothing but a small property of my own, and it's in disrepair. My only hope to save it is to wed an heiress who doesn't mind marrying a man with nothing."

His confession eased her mind, and she pulled up an empty crate, sitting down upon it. "Is that why you came to Castle Keyvnor? Are you in search of a bride?"

"I am," he agreed. He pulled up a crate of his own. "It sounds rather mercenary, but I am in need of a wealthy one."

"I c-can understand that." Her teeth still wouldn't stop chattering, despite the warmth of his coat.

"Are you all right, Miss Hawkins?" His voice held kindness, and he drew his crate beside hers.

"Just fr-freezing," she admitted. "But your coat makes it bearable. I got wet from the rain, and I can't s-stop shivering."

He fell silent a moment and regarded her. In the dim candlelight, his expression turned thoughtful. "Would you consider me a friend, Miss Hawkins?"

She didn't know what to make of that question. "I hardly know you."

"Yes, but would you agree with me when I say I have no intention of harming you?"

"Of course." To the contrary, he had done everything possible to ensure that she was safe and protected.

"Good." With that, he drew his arms around her. "Then trust that this means nothing."

With his arms around her, he cocooned her in his body heat. Logically, she understood that he was trying to prevent her from being cold. But never before had she been in a man's embrace. She could have pulled away—and he would have allowed this—but the comfort of his touch was undeniable.

Jane rested her hands against his chest and accepted the warmth. It should have embarrassed her, but instead, she wanted to draw closer. The scent of his skin and the hard planes of his body made her fully aware of this man. Never before had she felt such a need to touch someone. His hand idly stroked her shoulder, and she gave in to her instincts, resting her cheek against his heartbeat. His arms relaxed against her, offering heat, and yet giving her the freedom to do as she chose.

"Thank you," she murmured, wanting to remain in his arms. "I was colder than I realized." Against her cheek, she felt his rapid heartbeat, and his arms tensed.

"You looked miserable," he admitted. "I thought it might help."

It had, more than he knew. But instead of warming only her body, he had also awakened a frozen part of her spirit. She had never embraced a man before, and now that she knew the sensation, she felt as if the ice had cracked apart, melting at the heat of his skin.

"Better?" he asked, as he started to pull back.

No, stay, she wanted to tell him. But it wasn't right at all to remain in his arms. With great reluctance, she let him draw away, but she kept her eyes locked upon him.

"What is it?" he asked quietly.

Jane let out a slight breath of air and mustered a chagrined smile. "That was the first time I was ever in a man's arms, except for my adopted father's." She crossed her arms beneath his coat. "It was nice."

He stiffened at her compliment, as if he didn't know quite how to respond. Then he admitted, "I've done many things in my life of which I am not proud. Many would not call me nice."

It sounded as if he were trying to dissuade her from thinking he was a good man, which was strange. "I would not call you wicked."

"Some used to call me the Devil of Lancaster," he confessed. With a wry grin, he added, "Do not ask me to tell you why."

But his warning only made her smile. Devil or not, he had proved himself to be trustworthy.

"I am glad that you were locked in here with me, Mr. Lancaster," she told him. "I think I would be crying right now, if you weren't here."

He reached out and touched her chin, gently caressing it with his thumb. "I'm glad you're not alone." A spiral of warmth slid over her skin, down to her womb. Deep inside, she felt a yearning, as if he were touching her intimately. Her breasts tightened against her chemise and corset, and she couldn't tear her gaze from him.

She didn't understand the feelings coursing through her, nor could she bring herself to pull away. Instead, she covered his hand with her own.

"Don't look at me like that, Miss Hawkins," he said softly. His voice was deep, but instead of warning her away, it attracted her. "You are a temptation I don't want to refuse."

He held her transfixed, and he framed her face with his hands. The sensation of his warm palms against her cheeks only magnified her yearning. She closed her eyes, feeling the rhythm of her own heartbeat against his breathing. In this darkness, she felt the boundaries slipping away until there was only the warmth of a man's touch upon her skin.

"Tell me not to kiss you," he said quietly. She couldn't bring herself to speak, for she wanted him to. She wanted to know what it was like to feel a man's mouth upon hers.

He leaned toward her, giving her every opportunity to escape. But she didn't move at all. When his mouth brushed against hers, she felt heat blazing over her skin. Without knowing why, she put her arms around him, pulling him closer.

The kiss transformed, and he deepened it, bringing her against him. "This wasn't my intention," he muttered, even as he kissed her harder. No longer did she feel cold, and the shudders that rippled across her body had nothing to do with the frigid air. Desire flooded through her, and he threaded his hands through her hair as he held her mouth captive.

She couldn't grasp a rational thought, but her breasts ached beneath her gown, rising against the damp fabric.

Her breath caught in her lungs, and when she opened to him, he slid his tongue within her mouth.

Dear God. She felt the invasion as surely as if he had claimed her body. Between her legs, she felt a swollen heat, the craving for a more intimate act.

And somewhere, deep inside, she realized that this was how her mother had been seduced. She had listened to the yearning of her body instead of her rational mind.

Jane knew if she didn't pull away, she would fall beneath this man's spell, allowing him any liberty he wished. She broke free of the kiss, feeling ashamed of the way she had offered herself to him. This never should have happened.

For a moment, there was only silence stretching between them. She didn't know what to say, and neither did he. They were saved from further conversation when there came the sound of a key turning in the lock.

"Go," she whispered to Mr. Lancaster, handing him his coat. He ducked behind a shelf of wine bottles, hiding himself from view, and the door opened.

"What's all this?" the housekeeper demanded. She frowned at Jane as if it were her fault that she was locked inside. "Why are *you* here?"

"I came in search of Lady Banfield," she explained, "and someone locked me inside."

The matron glared at her. "What nonsense. You were trying to steal wine for yourself. Admit it."

Stealing wine? The woman's accusation infuriated her, and Jane stood. "I am telling you the truth, and you've no right to insinuate that I would be here for any other reason." Without a word, she moved past the housekeeper, walking up the stairs that led up to the wooden door. Belatedly she froze, realizing that she had left Mrs. Bray alone where Devon might be discovered. From behind her, she heard the housekeeper take a bottle from one of the wine racks and follow her. Dear God, she hoped Mrs. Bray had not seen him. She waited for the woman to return to the stairs and slipped behind her to ensure the door was left open a crack for Devon.

When she stepped outside, the rain had stopped. Hazy sunlight filtered through the clouds, and droplets of water glistened upon the grass.

As she returned to the house, her face burned with embarrassment when she thought of kissing Devon Lancaster. But she could lay no blame at his feet. *She* had invited the kiss, and it had shattered her to the core.

He had been open with her from the beginning. He could never marry a woman like herself, and he needed an heiress to restore his estate. But now she was left with an even greater fear—that if she didn't shut down her instinctive feelings, she would end up seduced and left alone.

Exactly like her mother.

Chapter Three

LATER THAT EVENING

Devon waited through supper, but there was no sign of Miss Hawkins. He had hoped to see her again after their captivity in the wine cellar, but she had not come down.

As for himself, he had been glad that no one had discovered them together. He had escaped the wine cellar several minutes after she'd left with the housekeeper, and it did not seem that anyone was aware that they were locked inside together.

Lady Marjorie joined him at the table, along with her sisters. When he asked her where Jane was, the young woman shrugged. "Jane took a tray in her room."

In other words, she was avoiding him. Devon reached for his glass, remembering the stolen moment in the wine cellar. Though he didn't know what had possessed him to kiss her, never had he imagined such a response. Her lips were soft, inviting him to take more. And when he'd given in to his urges, kissing her hard, he'd been stunned by her open response. This was a woman of hidden passion, one whose innocence veiled her innermost needs.

41

He had kissed many women, and there was no secret about his reputation in London. They called him the Devil of Lancaster instead of Devon. He had accepted many women into his bed, none of them a virgin, but never had any woman affected him the way this one did.

Her innocent sighs and the way she'd clung to him had pushed him past the edge of control. He'd wanted to pull her onto his lap, to kiss her until she was breathless, loosening the ties of her gown until he could taste her bare skin.

It was possibly a stroke of good luck that she had not come to dinner, for he likely would have been staring at her during the entire meal. Yet, he knew better than to court this woman. Jane might receive a small inheritance from the late earl, but it was unlikely there would be much of anything.

Devon wished he were in a position to marry a woman of his choosing. But he had tenants who were relying upon him to marry well. He had no right to disregard their needs or the needs of the estate.

He ought to turn his attentions to the new Lord Banfield's daughters. Lady Marjorie and Lady Tamsyn were both beautiful young women, along with their sisters, Morgan, Gwyn, and Rose. All of the young women would have handsome dowries and would be suitable.

And yet, none captivated him in the way Jane Hawkins did. She might seem like a quiet young woman, hardly more than a shy wallflower. But there was far more to her than anyone knew.

"We will play cards later," Lady Marjorie was saying. "If you want to see Jane, I'll see to it that she comes."

"Does she like whist?" he asked.

"Jane is quite a good card player. I'll warn you

now—you should never wager against her. She might seem to be no one of consequence, but she could easily win every last coin before you realize it."

There was great irony in a vicar's daughter beating everyone at cards, but it didn't surprise him. Miss Hawkins struck him as a woman of intelligence, despite her quiet demeanor.

"Are we playing for stakes, then?" He had little to wager, but if Miss Hawkins was coming to play, he intended to partner with her, if at all possible.

"Why not?" Lady Marjorie answered. "Or we might play for the fun of it." She leaned closer and sent him a conspiratorial smile. "Are you thinking of getting better acquainted with her?"

He knew exactly what she was implying but didn't know how to answer that. "We have spoken on a few occasions. I would consider her a friend."

Lady Marjorie sighed. "Jane deserves a happy ending to her life. She's had so many hardships, but I adore her."

He finished his meal and excused himself from the table while the ladies departed. His thoughts were heavy as he walked along the hallway, for he *did* like Jane Hawkins. If she were an heiress, he would have pursued her without question. It bothered him to recognize that money would affect his decisions so strongly. As the youngest son, he had no means of creating his own fortune—at least, not yet.

He had come to Castle Keyvnor in search of a bride…but instead, he'd come to realize that what he truly needed was a purpose. He had property of his own and would it not be better to build a fortune to go with it? Then he would be free to pursue whatever woman he wished.

He started to join the others, when the frigid gust of air surrounded his shoulders once more.

Enough of the ghost, already. He had other plans in mind. But this time, when he turned around, he caught a glimpse of a man dressed in Tudor attire with a ruff around his neck. He had reddish hair, a beard, and blue eyes. The ghost carried a lute under one arm and pointed down the hallway.

Devon blinked, only to find that the man had vanished. It was possible that he'd imagined all of it. And yet, the details of the ghost were vivid within his mind.

He questioned whether or not to obey the ghost's directions. Why should he care whether or not the man wanted him to go down the hall?

And yet, Jane had not come to dinner. Someone had locked her in the wine cellar earlier, and she might still be in danger.

He saw no alternative but to follow.

After she had finished the dinner on her tray, Jane changed back into the dark blue serge long-sleeved gown. The white gown was still damp from the rain, and the very sight of it reminded her of being locked in the wine cellar with Devon Lancaster.

She was still angry at herself for letting him kiss her. It had been an impulse and one that would not happen again. He had been very clear that he needed to wed an heiress—and she was not at all wealthy. It might be best to wear this gown and remind him of that fact. If nothing else, it would help her to keep him at a distance.

Marjorie had asked her to join in a game of cards, and Jane decided it was just the distraction she needed. She left her room and closed the door behind her, walking toward the stairs.

From below, she heard the sounds of conversation. And there was a high-pitched noise coming from outside. At first, she ignored it, but for a moment, it almost sounded like a woman screaming.

The hair on the back of her neck rose up. *It could be the ghost of Lady Banfield.* Her mind considered the idea, then discarded it. She truly didn't believe in spirits, despite what she'd heard at breakfast. But worse was the idea that another young woman might be in trouble. A man had locked her into the wine cellar. Why not someone else?

Jane walked toward an open window and peered outside. The noise definitely seemed to be coming from one of the castle turrets. She decided it was best to go and investigate, though she needed to find someone to accompany her. Devon Lancaster would go along if she asked, but she didn't want him to feel obligated. There might be a footman who could watch over her. Or better, she could tell someone what she had heard.

Jane hurried down the stairs and along the hallway, moving in the direction of the turret. When she drew closer, the wailing grew louder. The woman sounded as if she were in a great deal of anguish, and the screams mingled with sobs.

This was more than tales of a ghost. The crying was quite clear, and *someone* was inside the turret.

Jane hesitated a moment, wondering if she dared to go closer. But how could she stand aside and pretend as if nothing was happening? Whoever was up there clearly needed help.

A serving maid passed through the hall, and Jane rushed toward her. "Excuse me. But…I heard a noise. I think someone needs help."

The maid stopped a moment, and said, "I'm sorry, miss, but I'm needed in the kitchen."

"But don't you hear the screaming?" As soon as Jane spoke of it, the sound abruptly stopped.

"I'm sure it's nothing, miss." The maid's expression remained disinterested, as if she heard the sound all the time. Was she ignoring it? It was impossible for her not to have heard the shrieking. But her behavior suggested that it was nothing out of the ordinary. Jane waited a moment, expecting to hear the wailing again, but there was nothing.

"If you'll excuse me, miss." The maid bobbed a curtsy and moved back in the direction of the kitchen.

Jane questioned whether or not to pursue the sound, but it was the clear the maid had no intention of investigating it. She paused at the bottom of the staircase and waited. Inwardly, she was torn on whether to abandon her search. In the end, she decided to walk up the staircase and listen to hear if she heard any further noises. It seemed a good compromise rather than to trespass where she wasn't wanted.

She walked up the first spiral staircase and then the second, pausing at each landing. At first, she heard nothing. But when she reached the last staircase, she heard the piercing scream, followed by wailing.

"He's dead. Oh God, my son is dead!"

The woman's shrieking sent a chill through her, and Jane froze in place. She remembered that Lady Banfield had lost her five-year-old son, and there were never any more children.

Was it possible that she could still be alive? Jane didn't believe such a notion, for everyone would know about it. Unless it truly *was* a ghost.

Every instinct warned her to flee, but her brain reminded her that ghosts were not real. If this truly was a flesh-and-blood person, it wasn't right to abandon a woman in need of help.

Jane lowered her head and continued up the stairs. From behind her, she heard rapid footsteps approaching.

"Get back!" a male voice snarled. Jane turned to see who it was, but before she could get a clear glimpse of the servant, he seized her arm and shoved her down the stairs. Her body jolted against the hard ridges of the wooden steps, and she tried to regain her footing. Instead, she tumbled hard until she reached the landing.

It hurt to breathe, and she gasped for air, for the wind had been knocked out of her. For a moment, she felt her ribcage, wondering if she had broken any bones.

"You will not go any further," the man shouted from the top of the stairs. Jane tried to catch a glimpse of the man's face, but there was no clear view of him. "If you dare to disturb her, I will kill you." He slammed the door and she heard a key turning in the lock.

A shiver crossed her spine at the threat. Was this the same man who had locked her in the cellar? His voice sounded the same. He was clearly trying to frighten her away from Castle Keyvnor—and if that was his intent, he was succeeding. She'd done nothing wrong and twice, someone had tried to hurt her. If she'd had the means to leave, she would have. There were secrets in this place, and somehow her life was bound up in those invisible bindings.

Jane sat up gingerly. It didn't seem that she had broken anything—but her body would have bruises for some time. She steadied herself and held on to the railing as she hoisted herself to her feet. The screaming had stopped, and she walked back downstairs, feeling shaken.

"Miss Hawkins," a voice called out. "Are you all right?"

She turned and saw Devon Lancaster approaching.

The moment she saw him, she felt the urge to weep in his arms. She wanted to feel his embrace and pour out her fears.

Instead, she squared her shoulders and joined him. "I—I think so."

He hurried to stand before her. "You look upset and frightened. Almost as if you've seen a ghost." His expression turned concerned, and he reached out to tuck a strand of hair behind her ear.

"Not a ghost. But someone who pushed me down the stairs." She kept her voice low and explained what happened. "I swear to you, I heard a woman screaming. I couldn't just walk away from a woman in trouble."

His face turned grim. "It might be that you *did* hear a ghost. I heard stories over dinner about the ghost of the late Lady Banfield."

"I heard the same during breakfast. But what sort of man would lock his wife away?"

He offered her his arm, and she took it, feeling comfort at his presence beside her. "I don't know. But if you want me to ask the servants about the noise in the turret, I can."

"I already tried, but the maid was ignoring it." She stopped walking a moment. "What I want is to leave this castle and not look back. From the moment I've arrived, it has brought me nothing but fear and danger."

"Will you let me guard you?" he asked quietly.

She wanted to say yes but questioned whether it was wise to spend time with this man. Whether or not he realized it, his very presence drew her closer. And both of them knew there could be nothing between them.

"I think I should make arrangements to go home," she countered.

"And what of Lady Marjorie? She will be remaining here, since Castle Keyvnor is to be her new home."

"For a time," Jane agreed. "But I always intended to go back."

"Stay a little longer," he urged. "You were meant to come here. You should find out why."

"And what if I do not want the answers?" It terrified her to think of who her father had been, or to discover why someone wanted her far from here.

He covered her hand with his gloved palm. "Running away won't change anything, Jane."

The use of her first name brought about an unexpected intimacy between them, but she said nothing to correct him.

"You're right." She rubbed at her bruised arms, wincing when she touched her ribs. "But I cannot ask you to be with me at every moment."

His expression turned thoughtful. "Believe me, it would not be a hardship." A sudden warmth suffused her at his words, and she reminded herself once again that they would be friends and nothing more.

When they reached the main hall, he paused a moment. "If you want me to escort you back to your room, I would be glad to. Or, if you would prefer to be surrounded by people, I understand there will be card games in the parlor."

The logical choice was to lie down and rest after she'd been shoved down the stairs. And yet, the idea of being alone in her room made her wary. Someone could still break inside, and there would be no one to hear her call out for help.

"I suppose I'll join the others in cards." At least then, she would be in a public place where no one could harm her.

"Lady Marjorie tells me that you are an outstanding whist player."

She wasn't about to boast so simply shrugged. "I

have played the game often." It was scandalous enough that she played cards in secret. Her adopted father would be outraged if he knew that she excelled at the games. But she'd always been able to use reasoning and memory to make decisions on when to play a trump.

"Would you like to be my partner?" he inquired.

"I don't believe that would be wise. If you are truly here to find a bride, you should use this as a chance to become better acquainted with a wealthy young lady. Not me."

They stopped in front of the parlor where men and women were beginning to choose partners. The ladies had paired up together and the gentlemen chose their own tables. It was safer that way, Jane thought. At least she would not have to worry about a pair of green eyes studying her with unconcealed interest.

And she could ignore the pounding of her own heart.

Devon played to win, much to his partner's delight. He and Teddy Lockwood played hand after hand, and it did seem that luck was with him tonight. Oddly enough, he was hardly paying any attention. Instead, he was staring across the room at Miss Hawkins, who appeared to be winning against her opponents.

Jane stood out from the other young ladies, not only because of her sensible dark blue gown, but also because of her severe updo. The other young women were beautifully dressed in silks with jewels adorning their throats and wrists. And yet, Jane's eyes gleamed with the spark of competition. Her cheeks were flushed and she had a small pile of coins before her.

"You have the devil's own luck it seems." Jack tossed in his hand of cards and glared at Devon.

"Perhaps I have a ghost whispering secrets in my ear." It wasn't true, but he didn't mind poking fun at his friend.

"Don't say ghost," Michael Beck complained.

"If I didn't know better, I'd swear that was true." Jack leaned back in his chair and shook his head at his partner.

"But before we start another hand," Michael began, "and before I lose more money, tell me what else you've learned about Miss Hawkins."

Devon didn't know why the sudden interest, but he straightened. "Why do you ask?" He felt a protective instinct toward Jane and didn't want either of the men eyeing her.

Michael reached for the cards and began shuffling the deck. "If she is indeed an heiress, you're not the only man here with an interest."

Beneath the table, his hands curled into fists. He didn't know what had provoked the surge of jealousy, but he didn't want anyone bothering Jane. His friends exchanged knowing looks, and Michael dealt the next hand.

"Don't even consider it," Devon warned. "She's a lady, one who deserves better than the likes of you." Or himself, if the truth be known. Still, he didn't want these men bothering her.

"Try not to kill them before we've finished the next hand," Teddy interrupted. "We *are* winning, after all." He picked up his cards and leaned back in his chair.

"Turn your attention back to Lady Cassandra and away from Miss Hawkins," Devon warned Jack. "And as for you—" He gave a hard stare to Michael "—find another heiress. Miss Hawkins doesn't believe she'll inherit much of anything."

Yet, even as he spoke the words, he had his doubts.

Anyone who would go to such lengths to drive Jane away from Castle Keyvnor—locking her in the wine cellar and pushing her down the stairs—had a strong reason. And he believed that it involved the secret of her father.

What if her father was supposed to be the true heir instead of Allan Hambly? It might change everything.

Devon didn't know what the reasons were, but he fully intended to protect Jane until the will was read. Only then would they know why someone was trying to harm her.

"You're still staring at her, Lancaster." Teddy pointed to the cards in front of Devon. "And it's your turn."

He was about to pick up his hand when he saw an older matron standing in front of Jane. The woman was chastising her for some reason, and Jane looked taken aback by her words. She stood from her chair, putting down her cards.

"I'll be back in a moment," Devon said, tucking a deck of cards into his coat pocket. He didn't know what was happening, but he crossed the room in a few paces before Jane could leave.

"Is everything all right?" he asked her quietly.

Jane was about to answer, but then the matron cut her off. "Of course not. Miss Hawkins clearly doesn't understand that gently bred women do not gamble."

"You've lost money, then?" he predicted.

The stout woman rested her hands upon her waist. "I would never consider wagering in cards. It's simply not done."

To Jane, Devon asked, "How much did she lose?"

She shrugged. "Her daughters, Lady Samantha and Lady Cassandra, played against Marjorie and me. We were only making small wagers."

"Any wagers at all are inappropriate," the woman insisted. "And if you were from a decent family, you would know this."

Jane's expression held a brittle smile, but she stood from the gaming table and excused herself, leaving the coins behind. "Marjorie, you can see to it that Lady Widcombe receives everything back."

Her face was flushed, but she strode toward the door. Devon tried to slow her down. "You aren't going to let her spoil your evening, are you?"

"I think my day was most thoroughly spoiled already." She moved past him and walked into the hallway. He followed while she hastened toward the stairs. Once she reached them, she stopped and regarded him. "What are you doing, Mr. Lancaster?"

"Exactly what I promised. I said I would ensure that you were safe. Unless you believe this staircase is safer than the last one?"

Her eyes filled with tears, and she rested her hands on the bannister. "I don't know what to think anymore. Right now I want to go cry in my room, but I don't think I can do even that."

He offered his handkerchief. "I could take you someplace safe, for now. Perhaps the library or even the chapel, if you like."

She dabbed at her eyes and nodded. "The library, then. But I want you to first ensure that there are no men lurking about. And I want the door to be propped open so we aren't locked inside."

"I heartily agree." He walked with her down the hallway, guiding her in the right direction. It was getting late, and the candlelight cast shadows against the lofted ceilings. Devon thought he caught a glimpse of the Tudor ghost smiling at them from high above the Hall. It was unnerving, but he tried to ignore it.

Right now, he wanted Jane's day to end better than it had begun. They continued walking through the hallway until they reached the library. Devon opened the door for her, and the moment Jane saw the interior, she smiled. The high ceiling was made of a rich wood with ribbed vaulting. Long wooden columns spanned the distance to the floor, and there was a second level of bookshelves with a walkway and balcony running down the length of the room.

"There must be hundreds of books in here," Jane breathed. She appeared delighted by the sight of them, and her tears were momentarily forgotten. For a few minutes, she browsed through the bookcases, and Devon noticed the arrival of the Tudor ghost. The spirit beamed at them, his blue eyes twinkling as he took a position on the second floor of the library. He rested his hands upon the balcony, as if enjoying a play.

Devon wasn't certain if Jane could even see the ghost but decided not to mention it. After everything that had happened, he didn't want her to be terrified of the meddling spirit.

"Feeling better?" he asked. Jane trailed her fingertips over the books and then turned back to face him.

"A little." She offered him his handkerchief back and admitted, "This has been the worst day I've ever had."

There were two wingback chairs beside one of the bookcases with a table between them. Devon motioned for her to sit down a moment, and then he withdrew the deck of cards he'd brought from the parlor. "Would you care to play a round of German whist?"

She studied him with an amused gaze. "Lady Widcombe said it's not ladylike to gamble."

"Only because her daughters were losing. I don't lose," Devon said.

As he'd hoped, her eyes lit up with the challenge. "Only because you've never played against me."

Devon began shuffling and dealing out the cards, and Jane glanced toward the door. "Do you suppose we ought to fetch a chaperone? It's not right to be alone. Perhaps we should get two more players."

He shrugged. "I wasn't planning to stay that long. Only for a few hands. But if you don't feel safe with me…"

Jane shook her head. "No, I suppose you're right. You've gotten me out of many scrapes thus far." She picked up her cards and studied them for a moment while he flipped up the trump card. He set the stack of undealt cards to the side

"Spades," he remarked. He studied her for any sort of reaction, but she appeared too interested in sorting her cards.

She led her first card, a queen of diamonds. He trumped it with a nine of spades. "My trick."

But she only gave him a slight smile. He collected the top card from the deck, and the game progressed round by round, until they were down to the last eight cards. She had played with strategy, discerning which were his weaker suits, until the deck was nearly gone. All the while, he could hardly take his gaze off her.

Jane lit up from within as she competed during the game. At one interval, she tucked one foot beneath her skirts, pondering her hand. She bit her lip, deciding which card to play, and the gesture drew his attention back to her mouth.

Which made him want to kiss her again.

Abruptly, she laid down the ace of spades. "You've lost, Mr. Lancaster."

"There are several more rounds," he countered, tossing away a two of spades. "It's not over yet." They both were tied with equal tricks taken. But for the life of him, he could barely remember which cards had been played. He'd been too distracted by her.

Jane smiled and laid down the king, queen, and jack of spades. "It is most definitely over. I win."

He tossed his hand and leaned back in the chair. "I would say we both won."

"How do you mean?" She gathered the cards and began to shuffle them.

"I made you smile again."

Her expression faltered, but then her mouth softened. "You did try to redeem my horrid day." She set aside the deck and added, "I never imagined it would be like this." He waited for her to continue, and she added, "I thought I could come to Castle Keyvnor and remain in the background where no one would notice me."

"Any man would notice you," Devon countered. "Unless he was dead."

At that, the ghost coughed heavily and shook his head. Devon had nearly forgotten about the specter, and he acknowledged, "Or even those who *are* dead. Perhaps the ghosts of this castle have noticed you."

Now the Tudor ghost smiled and began to preen. He pulled out a lute and plucked a few strings. Jane leaned her head to the side. "Do you hear that?"

"Hear what?" He wanted to know exactly what she was sensing, for truthfully, he had no idea whether the ghost was real or not.

"The music." Her face furrowed, and she listened harder. "I can't tell where it's coming from. It almost seems to be coming from the top floor of the library. Is someone there?"

"I don't see anyone." The last thing he wanted was to terrify Jane with the vision of a matchmaking specter. Devon sent a pointed look toward the ghost, who then disappeared inside one of the bookcases.

"It reminds me of Renaissance music," Jane said. "A little old fashioned, but lovely." Her face brightened, and the face of the Tudor ghost emerged from the wood. He appeared quite pleased with himself.

A strange idea occurred to him, but Devon asked, "Would you care to dance?"

"What, here?" Jane laughed and glanced around.

He took a step closer and held out his hand. "Why not? Since you've had such a difficult day. It might be fun."

Jane was still amused by the idea but shrugged. "All right, then." She took his hand, and he put his other hand at her waist. The ghost played a more lilting song, and Devon led her into a country dance. She curtseyed to him, and they promenaded the length of the library. They walked in circles around one another while the ghost's music grew more lively. Devon spun her around, and she couldn't help but laugh.

"Never in my life have I danced in a library," she admitted, as they strolled in the opposite direction.

"You dance very well for a vicar's daughter."

"It's Marjorie's fault. She made me come to dancing lessons with her, but sometimes I had to take the gentleman's part. If I make a mistake, that's why."

"You dance very well, Jane."

She faltered a moment and chided him, "You should call me Miss Hawkins."

"I should, but I don't want to. And you may call me Devon." He spun her again, and this time, she caught his shoulders for balance, laughing again.

"I will not," she argued. But she was still smiling at him. "I'm getting dizzy with all this spinning."

The music ended, and another tune began, this one mournful and melodic. He stopped dancing but continued to hold on to her waist. Jane was smiling, but when she looked into his eyes, her smile faded.

"Why are you staring at me?" she murmured.

"You know why." His hand moved up her spine, and he wanted nothing more than to kiss her again. He wanted to cup her nape, drawing those soft lips to his, and falling beneath her spell. Her blue eyes held uncertainty, but he leaned in and stole a kiss anyway.

"Mr. Lancaster, don't," she protested. "I am not the woman you want."

"Devon," He corrected. "And you are exactly the woman I want. How can you doubt that?" He kissed her again, tasting the sweetness of her tongue and drawing her body against his. He continued to move with her, leading her into the scandalous waltz while the music played above them.

For a moment, she kissed him back, and that was enough to push him past the edge. His hunger roared within him, to touch this beautiful woman and make her feel the same way he did.

But a second later, she pushed him back. "No. I can't do this." Her eyes held fear, and she reached trembling fingertips to her swollen lips.

"Why not? You don't seem to mind it when I kiss you."

"Because you're not going to marry a woman like me," she said quietly. "We both know it."

He couldn't say anything in reply, for she might be right. There was no way of knowing what would happen between them. But he didn't want to admit that.

"We've only known each other two days," he said. "It's too soon to worry about marriage or anything of that nature. Is it not enough to get to know one another?"

"Not like this." She rested her palms upon his beating heart. "I cannot let you kiss me again."

"You don't have to be afraid of me," he said. "I would never touch you against your will." Never in his life had he harmed a woman, and he wasn't about to start now.

"I'm not afraid of you," Jane whispered. "I'm afraid of myself." She lowered her gaze, revealing her shyness. "When I let you touch me, I lose sight of everything right and wrong. It's as if the ground beneath my feet falls away. And I understand how my mother was seduced. I don't want to be like her. I can't." With that, she stepped away from him. "I will not let myself fall into the same temptation she did."

"I wasn't seducing you." He didn't want her to think that he was going to push her too far. "It was only a kiss."

She took another step toward the door and then turned back. "To you, it was. But to me, it was much, much more."

After she had gone, Devon glanced up at the ghost, who appeared sympathetic. "The music was a nice touch. But it seems I've made a mess of things."

"Aye, you have," the ghost replied. "Desire doth clip the wings of the heart when it is forced too soon."

"What is your name?" Devon asked. "Were you the one beheaded in the courtyard?"

The ghost glowered at him. "I am Benedict. And thou shouldst not ask questions about a man's death. It is quite rude."

"I suppose it *is* rather personal," Devon agreed. "Well, what now, Benedict? Should I find another lady instead? This one doesn't appear to want me."

The ghost floated down to the first level. "A woman's words show not what it is her heart. And only a fool would walk away from one so fair."

"I couldn't agree more."

CHAPTER FOUR

The next morning, Jane spied Marjorie's father, Lord Banfield, walking through the garden. Right now, she needed answers that only he could give. He must have known who her father was if he had arranged to bring her to Castle Keyvnor.

He passed by the hedge maze, and she hurried to catch up to him. "Lord Banfield, might I speak with you for a moment?"

The earl stopped and turned around. "Miss Hawkins," he greeted her. "Is something the matter?"

Jane caught up to him and asked, "I wanted to ask you about what happened at breakfast yesterday morning. Mr. Hunt seemed to think I was here for the will reading." She paused a moment. "But that's not at all why I came. I thought I was meant to be Marjorie's companion."

His face turned troubled, and he shrugged. "I can't really say, Miss Hawkins. Mr. Hunt will handle those matters. It's likely nothing of concern." He started to walk toward the maze, but she cut him off.

"But it is." Jane wasn't about to let him leave without the answers she wanted. "Someone locked me in the wine cellar yesterday. And later, a servant knocked me down the stairs. It might have been the same man, but I cannot be sure."

She had his attention now, and Lord Banfield appeared shocked. "Why would anyone do such a thing?"

Jane shook her head. "I thought you might know. But whoever did it is trying to force me to leave Castle Keyvnor." She explained what had happened in the turret about the woman and the screaming.

He paled. "I think you may have been in the wrong place at the wrong time."

"And what about the wine cellar? Why would anyone care about someone like me, enough to threaten me like this? Or push me down the stairs?" She shook her head. "It has to do with my father. I'm certain of it."

She took a deep breath and studied Allan Hambly. Although they had never been close, she knew he'd been responsible for giving her to her adopted parents. "Who was he, Lord Banfield? I must know."

The earl regarded her for a long moment. "I suppose you do have the right. But…it is very complicated."

She walked alongside him as he led her through the garden. When he was certain that no one was eavesdropping, he said, "Your father came to visit Regina and I, many years ago. He and his wife were estranged."

A flush came over her cheeks when she caught his meaning. "So his wife did not come with him, did she?"

"No. And from the moment he set eyes upon your mother, he was enchanted by her. Emily Hawkins was a governess for a family who lived in the townhouse next to ours. I don't even remember why she came to our house that day, but from the moment he saw her, it was as if he were under a spell. He wasn't supposed to stay long with us, but his visit extended for a fortnight."

"He betrayed his wedding vows," Jane whispered. "And my mother allowed it."

"I think she was not accustomed to such attention. He gave her jewels and baubles. Sent her flowers and took her out driving." The earl's tone held remorse. "She made him feel young again."

At that, her stomach twisted, and she feared what he would say then. "You never told me his name. Who was he?"

Lord Banfield met her gaze squarely. "He was Jonathan Hambly, the late Earl of Banfield. And you are his only surviving daughter."

Devon joined his friends for a game of billiards in the early afternoon, but his mind was not on the game. He knew that he was spending too much time with Jane Hawkins, but he hardly cared. With each moment he spent at her side, he liked her more. She fit into his arms and it felt natural to spend time with her. And most of all, he felt as if he could speak openly with her, without any pretenses.

But he knew how badly his family would react if he told them he wanted to court a vicar's daughter. They would ridicule him and cast disparaging remarks about Jane. She would be miserable, and he didn't want others to look down on her.

Regardless of her birth, she had an inner strength that attracted him. Most women would have required smelling salts after yesterday's events. Instead, Jane had managed to overcome her fears, dancing with him in the library.

Until he'd kissed her again.

He'd been unable to resist her, needing to feel the

softness of her mouth beneath his. Every time he touched her, he felt the need to bring her closer. She'd said that she was afraid of herself, afraid of becoming like her mother.

Whereas he was afraid to let her go.

Devon knew Jane was unlike other women. And he had a feeling that from now until the day he married, he would be unable to get her out of his mind. She haunted him, just as surely as the ghosts haunted this castle.

He took a shot with his cue ball, but missed the red ball badly. His friend, Jack, narrowed his gaze. "You're out of sorts, aren't you, Lancaster?"

"I've a lot on my mind." He waited for Jack to take his turn at billiards.

After the soft clack of the ivory ball, his friend regarded him. "This is about the woman, isn't it? The one I thought was a servant."

"She's a vicar's daughter," he told him.

Jack let out a sigh. "Out of all the women here, why her? She's not at all the sort of lady you wanted. Quite ordinary, isn't she?"

Devon's fists clenched. "I might say the same about Lady Cassandra."

There was no mistaking the sudden rage on St. Giles's face. "If you did, I'd skewer you with this cue, Lancaster."

Devon set his cue down and let out a gruff sigh. "No need for us to fight about it. It seems we're both having ill luck with women." He had lost the game to Jack, and when his friend invited him for another, Devon declined.

Jack picked up the ivory balls and set them back into a box. "I don't think the problem is finding a woman. It's a matter of convincing her that we are honorable men."

Devon snorted at the irony of Jack's statement. More

likely Jane was convinced he had no intentions toward her, save seduction. Even if she did turn out to be an heiress, she would believe he wanted her only for her money.

Did it truly matter whether she was an heiress? His property was humble, as was the small house upon it. He'd always imagined himself marrying a woman who would help him restore the house and lands, building them into a grand estate.

But perhaps he was simply trying to prove something to his brothers—that despite being the youngest, he was a man of worth. And yet, he was trying to rely on someone else to build his fortune. It wasn't right.

His mind was burdened with heavy thoughts, and he poured himself a glass of brandy. Both he and Jane were cut from the same cloth—neither one with a fortune— and neither one daring to reach for what they truly wanted.

He finished his brandy and set the glass aside. In the morning, he would talk to her again and discover whether there was any chance at all for them.

It was difficult to avoid Devon Lancaster, but Jane had managed it by going on an outing to the local village of Bocka Morrow. The idea of escaping the castle, even for a few hours, was a welcome one. There were several young women who joined Marjorie and her, including Lady Samantha, Lady Claire—whom she had not met before—and a maid. One of the older footmen accompanied them into the village, though truthfully Jane doubted if Bronson could do much to defend them. Several times, she glanced behind and saw that he had a sour expression on his face as if he had better things to do than accompany a group of ladies shopping.

The steep walk downhill to the fishing village was slightly perilous, given the rain from the day before. Jane was careful with her footing, for the cobblestone streets were slick. The scent of fish was redolent in the air, and she wrinkled her nose.

"I'm not certain there will be any shops here," she told Marjorie. "It looks very small." Even the lanes were narrow, hardly large enough for a cart and horse to pass through. The overhanging roofs did offer shelter, in case the rain returned.

They passed by an inn called The Mermaid's Kiss, and Jane drew her shawl around her shoulders while the ladies gossiped. Right now, she hadn't said much to anyone, for her mind was still spinning from Lord Banfield's revelation.

She was the illegitimate daughter of the late earl. The knowledge staggered her with a blend of emotions. She would never know her father, and part of her was angry with him for seducing her mother. Why had Emily succumbed to the affections of an older man who was still married? Had Jonathan ever known she existed? Had Lord Banfield told him anything at all?

He must have, if she was in the will. Her stomach twisted with nerves, not because of any possible inheritance, but because it would make her into a spectacle. Everyone would know she was born out of an affair, and others would resent any portion she received.

But someone else knew the secret, and that someone wanted her gone. The easy way out was to leave Castle Keyvnor. And yet, that was the coward's path.

If her father had seduced and abandoned her mother, then he *did* owe Emily something. He had wronged her, and Jane only wished her mother were alive to receive that portion.

It would be small, no doubt, but that didn't matter. She would use it to repay her adopted parents for taking care of her all these years. John and Mary had loved her as their own child, and she wanted to ensure that they had enough to live in comfort for the remainder of their days.

"Oh look," Marjorie breathed, pointing to one of the apothecary shops. "Let's go inside."

Jane had no idea why her friend would want to visit the apothecary, but she shrugged. It was one of the few shops in the village, so that was likely why. She followed her inside, and the moment they entered the shop, the scent of herbs enveloped them. Jane saw bunches of rosemary and sage hanging from the ceiling, and along the back wall were rows of jars.

She was expecting to see a man, but instead, an older woman smiled and greeted them. Her long black hair was streaked with gray and it hung across her shoulders. Her skin was pale and wrinkled, but it was her hands that drew Jane's attention. She caught a glimpse of painted blue symbols upon the woman's fingers and knuckles. The ancient markings both fascinated and frightened her.

"Are you the apothecary?" Marjorie asked with a smile.

The old woman shook her head. "No, my father was. He taught me the healing arts, and I have been working here since I was a young girl. I am Brighid."

The shop door swung open, and a young woman with unruly strawberry blond curls entered. "Hello, Elethea." She nodded toward the woman in greeting. Then Brighid's kindly smile returned to Jane. "Is there anything I can help you find, ladies?"

"In a little while, perhaps." Marjorie walked over to a basket filled with bars of soap. She picked one up and smelled it. "Oh, this is heavenly. Jane, come and see what you think."

She took the bar of soap and the moment she inhaled the scent, it reminded her of an exotic moonlit garden. The floral aroma seemed almost sensual, and it took an effort for her to set it down.

"It is made from a rare jasmine plant," Brighid said. "It also contains sandalwood, orange essence, primrose, rose, and cinnamon oils." With a glance back at Jane, she added, "It would suit you very well, miss. The soap is very fine in quality, and the women who have used it have told me that their husbands...*enjoy* the aroma."

Jane wasn't quite certain what the woman meant by that, but she did love the perfume of the soap. She couldn't help but touch it once again. There was a softness to the texture, one that made her wish she could buy it. "It is wonderful," she agreed, tracing the surface of the soap. It was so very different from the hard lye soap she was accustomed to. But then, she couldn't afford small luxuries like this.

Brighid handed a different bar of soap to Marjorie. "And for you, I suggest this one. It has stronger notes of rose and similar ingredients."

Marjorie sniffed the second bar and nodded. "Oh, you're right. I do like this very much." She handed it over to Jane, who detected the blend of rose and cinnamon. "Isn't it delicious?"

Some of the other ladies were looking at packets of herbal tea, and Jane saw Lady Claire speaking with Elethea, though she could not say what they were talking about. She waited for them to finish their purchases, and to her surprise, she saw Marjorie hand both bars of soap to the healer. "We'll take them both. Jane, you may have the jasmine one."

"Very good," the old woman said. She wrapped each bar of soap in brown paper and tied one with a green ribbon and the other with rose.

"Marjorie, truly, it's not necessary."

"It will be my gift to you. After all, I dragged you across Cornwall. It's the least I can do." She handed over the bar of soap with a broad smile.

"I would advise you both to be very careful when you use the soap," Brighid warned. "The perfume may draw the attention of a particular gentleman." Her gaze turned to the footman, and she narrowed her eyes. Bronson folded his arms and glared right back at her. Jane hid her smile, for she doubted if any soap could ever draw the attention of a man like him. He was nearly old enough to be her grandfather.

"Excellent," Marjorie declared. "That is exactly what I was hoping for." Dropping her voice to a whisper, she said, "Only if I can find a handsome one who suits me well."

Jane tucked the bar of soap into her reticule and quietly thanked her friend. "You didn't have to do this, Marjorie. But I love the soap very much."

Her friend brightened and linked her arm with Jane's. "We are going to have a grand time today. And perhaps after we have a meal, we might go in search of the gypsies. I've heard that Lady Charlotte had her fortune told."

Jane remembered meeting Lady Charlotte earlier. The young woman was exuberant and charming, and Jane had liked her very much. But the idea of seeking out gypsies to have her fortune told was not at all appealing. Truth to tell, she didn't think they would find anything good about her future.

"Perhaps tomorrow," she said to Marjorie. "It's

getting late." And tomorrow she would find a reason not to go.

"All right." Her friend didn't seem deterred at all. "I am starving. We should go and get something to eat. Perhaps at the inn we passed earlier."

The others agreed, except for Lady Claire, who had an errand to run and departed with her maid and Elethea. Jane went along to the inn, though she wasn't particularly hungry. Right now, she felt distracted more than anything else.

She felt the outline of the bar of soap through her reticule and decided that tonight she would take a hot bath and enjoy the soft lather. Just thinking of the relaxing water brought a smile to her face. But as she held the bar, a sudden image came over her, of warm skin and slick water. She imagined a man's hands moving over her, washing her shoulders...his broad hands slipping down to her breasts.

The jolt of desire caught her by surprise, and she dropped her reticule on the cobbled streets. Her cheeks burned as she picked it up, but she recalled the healer's warning that women's husbands *enjoyed* the soap.

Oh dear. She feared she now understood exactly what that meant.

After luncheon, Jane felt terribly awkward when, once again, Marjorie paid for her food. She slowed her pace after they left The Mermaid's Kiss and let the others continue on the steep road leading back to Castle Keyvnor. The footman kept a slight distance away from them, but he kept guard.

"Marjorie," Jane said quietly. "Truly, you don't have

to pay for everything. It makes me uncomfortable." They had been friends long enough that she could be wholly honest with her.

But Marjorie got a mischievous look in her eyes. "Mr. Hunt didn't tell you, did he?"

"Tell me what?"

Marjorie linked her arm in Jane's and said, "You must promise not to say anything. But I heard that you're to receive a very large portion from the late Lord Banfield. Enough to make you a true heiress! Isn't that wonderful?"

A sinking feeling caught in her stomach, and Jane couldn't quite find the words to respond. Her friend blinked a moment and said, "Jane, are you not feeling well? I've just told you that you're to inherit a large portion, and you're not delighted by this?"

She hesitated, wondering if she dared to tell Marjorie the truth. "Did he tell you why?"

Her friend shook her head. "But I still don't understand why you aren't thrilled by this." She eyed her more closely. "You know the reason, don't you? And you haven't told me your secret."

Jane let out a sigh. "I only found out earlier today." Marjorie would be hurt if she didn't tell her, so she confessed, "Lord Banfield told me who my real father is."

Her friend brightened at the news and leaned closer. "Tell me everything."

"It seems that...my mother had an affair with Jonathan Hambly, the late Earl of Banfield, after his wife went mad. She became pregnant with me, but he could never acknowledge me as his daughter." Jane lifted her gaze to Marjorie. "He may be providing for me now, but it won't stop the scandal. Everyone will know that my mother was ruined by him."

Marjorie linked her arm in Jane's, her face sympathetic. "I do understand. But you are not at fault for his choices. And I, for one, am glad that you will receive part of his fortune. You deserve it, Jane."

Just then, the first raindrops began to fall. Bronson had brought two umbrellas. He hurried over to Lady Samantha, and then opened another umbrella to shielded Jane and Marjorie from the rain.

"You are an angel, Bronson," Marjorie proclaimed. Jane smiled at him gratefully, but he still did not respond with pleasantries—a grunt was his only answer.

Lady Samantha hurried up the embankment, muttering an unladylike curse when her footing slipped. She was farther ahead than the rest of them, trying to get out of the rain with the maid. In another minute, they saw she had nearly reached the castle entrance.

"We'll have to be careful," Marjorie warned. "It's very slippery along that pathway." She took slow steps, trying to avoid the mud.

Jane followed her example, but then the footman lost his balance. The umbrella went toppling from his hand, and he grabbed hold of her, trying to break his fall. Jane went skidding down the hillside, landing hard.

She winced at the realization that the muddy stains would never come out of her gown, and it was one of the nicer ones she owned.

"Jane, are you all right?" Marjorie asked.

"I'm fine. But I'm not so certain about Bronson." The older footman was on his hands and knees, facing downward. Jane tried to get up from the mud and asked, "Are you all right, Mr. Bronson?"

He gave no answer, but kept his head lowered. Beneath his breath, he appeared to be muttering something, but she couldn't quite tell what it was.

"Marjorie, come and help me with him." Her friend took careful steps down the hill until she reached the footman's side.

"Bronson, we're going to help you stand up." Jane moved to his right side and told Marjorie, "You take the left side."

But the moment she touched his shoulders, his fist shot toward Marjorie's face. Her friend let out a cry of pain before Bronson struck her again and she fell silent. Jane screamed, but he jerked her to her feet, clamping his hand over her mouth. His skin smelled of dirt and rain, and she was horrified to realize that this had all been a ruse.

"You aren't supposed to be here," he growled.

Dear God, she knew that voice. Panic clawed at her throat when she realized that *he* was the one who had locked her in the wine cellar and tried to throw her down the stairs. But why? What had she ever done to Bronson?

He kept his hand over her mouth, dragging her off the path and toward the edge of the hillside overlooking the sea. Below her, Jane saw waves swirling against the rocks, the foam circling the surface like boiling water.

She struggled against him, and he tightened his grip. "Stop fighting. It will all be over soon. She'll never know about you."

Over soon? And who was he talking about? His words spurred her harder, and she struggled with all her strength, kicking at him and trying to free herself. She would *not* stand here and let this madman throw her off a cliff.

Back on the pathway, she saw Marjorie standing immobile. If Bronson saw her, he might turn his anger toward her friend. Jane tried to point toward the castle, hoping her friend would understand her silent plea.

Go and bring back help.

It was pouring down rain and there was no sign of Jane. Devon knew she had gone to Bocka Morrow with a small group from the castle, but it seemed that the others had already returned.

Everyone except Lady Marjorie and Jane, that is. He asked if anyone had seen the two, and Lady Claire admitted, "They *were* just behind me. I know Lady Marjorie was talking about the gypsy camp. They might have gone back to look for it. She said she wants to have her fortune told tomorrow. But don't worry, they had Bronson to guide them back."

It should have reassured him, but with the terrible weather, Devon wasn't so certain. Every instinct warned him to go after Jane and find her.

He gave orders for his coat, hat, and an umbrella. Before the servant arrived, he felt frigid air settling around his shoulders. Devon glanced up and when the cold retreated, he saw the ghost, Benedict. The specter grimaced and pointed toward the door. It seemed that his worries were founded, and once the servant returned with his coat, he hurried outside. The ghost led him in the direction of the path toward Bocka Morrow. The hillside was slick from the rain, but he allowed the ghost to guide him.

Just then, he saw Lady Marjorie running toward him. Her bonnet was gone, and her hair was soaked around her shoulders. Mud coated her gown, and her eyes gleamed with panic. "Jane needs help. Please hurry!"

She tried to run back, but her footing slipped, and she

hit the ground hard. "Don't worry about me—just go! I'll get more help."

He obeyed, following the path until he saw Bronson holding Jane a few steps away from the edge of the cliff. She was fighting to free herself, but the footman was standing behind her with one arm across her throat, the other around her waist.

Devon didn't hesitate, but ran as hard as he could, heedless of the rain and the muddy path. "Let her go, Bronson." The footman was muttering to himself, and he couldn't quite make out the words. Devon took a few steps closer, seeing the wild fear in Jane's eyes.

"You have no reason to harm her. She's done nothing to you."

"She was born," Bronson shot back. "She never should have been alive. Not when my mistress tried for so many years to have another child."

Devon took a few steps closer, trying not to enrage the footman further. "I think you have Jane confused with someone else. She's the daughter of a vicar."

"She's a bastard daughter, that's what she is." The footman's eyes gleamed with hatred, and he glanced up at the turret. "My mistress lost her only son. Grieved for him and tried everything to have another. But Lord Banfield betrayed her. He went to another woman." He tightened his arm, and Jane gasped for air, trying to push him away.

Devon knew he had only seconds to save her life. The footman had lost his grasp on reality and would not be swayed with words. "You would punish the child for her father's sins?"

"My mistress *cannot* learn that this woman exists. She has been through enough pain. I will not stand by and let this...*nobody* inherit. I have stood by Lady Banfield all these years as her loyal servant. She must never know the truth." He stared back at the castle, his gaze resting upon one of the turrets.

He was speaking about a dead woman as if she were still alive. Devon realized that Bronson had likely been in love with Lady Banfield, but his mind had twisted the past and present together. And whether there was any truth to his words didn't matter—all Devon's focus was on saving Jane's life.

Bronson started to move toward the edge, and Devon closed the distance, seizing the man and throwing him to the ground. Jane landed beneath the footman, and it took all Devon's strength to drag the footman's hands away from her throat. He punched the man in the jaw, pouring his frustration and fury into the fight. Bronson was strong, in spite of his age, but Devon was faster.

He ripped the man free, forcing him away from Jane. The man swung his fist, and Devon ducked the blow, crushing his own punch into Bronson's stomach. He didn't hold back, but when he aimed another blow, the footman tried to scramble away. Bronson slipped, and he skidded backward, striking his head against a stone as he fell. He was motionless, and Jane paled.

"Is he dead?"

Devon went to check, but there was still a pulse. "No, he's unconscious." He stepped back and helped Jane to her feet. "What about you? Did he hurt you?"

She touched her throat, and he saw that her hands were shaking. "A little bruised, but nothing serious." With a rueful smile, she added, "And covered in mud."

He cared nothing for that but crushed her into his embrace. Her arms hugged him tightly, and a moment later, he heard servants approaching, along with Lord Banfield and Marjorie.

"What has happened?" the earl demanded, eyeing the fallen body of Bronson.

Devon explained, keeping Jane's hand in his. As he finished his tale, Jane said, "Mr. Lancaster saved my life, Lord Banfield. I am very grateful to him."

Marjorie rushed forward and hugged Jane tightly. "I was so afraid for you. I didn't want to leave you with that madman."

"I'm glad you did. You could not have saved me from him." To Devon, Jane added, "Thank you for coming for me."

He lifted her hand to his mouth. "I would never let anything happen to you."

The earl glanced at the way they were holding hands, and Devon stood his ground, letting the man know of his interest in Jane. Even though she was safe, his heart was still racing at the thought of what could have happened to her. She had been in true danger, and the footman could easily have thrown her over the side of the cliff. He touched his hand to the small of her back, so thankful she was all right.

"Let us go back inside," Lord Banfield said. "Jane, you will want some hot tea and clean clothing."

"And a bath, if it's not too much trouble," she pleaded. Her arms and face were caked in mud, along with her hair. Devon spied her fallen bonnet and reticule on the ground a few feet away, and he motioned for a servant to fetch them.

"Of course," the earl said. "I will see to it."

Devon helped her walk up the steep pathway leading back to the castle, and he saw the faint outline of Benedict. *I am very grateful, my friend,* he thought silently.

The ghost tipped his velvet cap and then vanished. Jane's hand tightened upon his, and she whispered, "Did you see—?"

"Yes," he answered with a smile. He rested his arm

around her waist, in the pretense of helping her keep her balance. The truth was, he needed to touch her, to ensure she was all right. If there were not so many people surrounding them, he would have claimed a kiss. Instead, he had to release her once they reached the safety of Castle Keyvnor.

But as Jane followed Marjorie down the hallway, she turned back to him. In her eyes, he saw the longing and gratefulness.

Thank you, she mouthed.

An hour later, Jane was seated in a wooden tub, scrubbing the mud from her body. She had sent the maid away, needing time to be alone. Her mind was still spinning from the earlier danger. Although she should now feel safe, since Bronson had been arrested and taken away from the castle, it was difficult to relax.

She decided to use the jasmine-scented soap, hoping the scent would help to calm her. The maid had left it near the tub, as she'd asked, and Jane unwrapped the brown paper. The moment she touched the soap, she felt her mood shift. She dipped it beneath the water and rubbed it between her palms to form a lather.

She washed herself, sliding the soap over her shoulders and arms. The aroma did seem to diminish her worries. Jane lathered the soap again and slid her wet palms over her breasts. Her nipples grew erect, and she felt an answering echo of need between her legs. She caught the trace scents of rose, primrose, and cinnamon mingling with the jasmine. Jane lifted her knee out of the water, washing it, and the moment she drew the soap over her leg, the feelings seemed to intensify.

Though she had meant only to wash herself, the

healer's warning came to mind, about a husband *enjoying* the soap. She knew that herbs could hold a strong effect, but it startled her that this soap was causing her to become aroused. Her body tingled in every place the lather had touched. When she rinsed the soap away, the restless feelings lingered.

For a moment, she closed her eyes, imagining Devon's face. He had gripped her tightly, as if she meant something to him. She was so thankful he had been there to save her from Bronson. And right now, she wanted so desperately to feel his kiss, to be in his arms.

Her breathing grew unsteady, and she reached for the soap again, allowing it to pull her beneath its invisible spell. She knelt down in the tub, soaping her bare skin. Every time she moved her hands over her breasts, she felt her body yearning for more. She traced the outline of her own nipples, shuddering as the heat rose over her.

God above, she didn't understand what was happening, but her need for Devon sharpened. She rinsed away the soap and reached for a towel, hoping the feelings would diminish. Instead, they intensified.

She dried herself and reached for the nightgown her maid had left. There was a tray of food on a table, for she had asked to dine alone. Everyone else was at dinner and would likely spend the evening gossiping about what had happened to her. She couldn't face them—not yet.

Jane put on the nightgown and walked toward the tray of food. A candle burned brightly in a brass chamberstick. As she sat down and toyed with the bread and soup, she found herself mesmerized by the patterned wallpaper. One of the seams didn't quite line up, and she walked over for a closer look. When she touched it, she heard a faint clicking noise. She pushed at the wall and was startled to see it open like a door into to a dark passageway. A cold gust seemed to press at her shoulders, and she picked up the chamberstick, shielding the candle with her hand as she stepped inside.

Where did the passageway lead? She followed the spiral stairs to a narrow corridor that stretched in both directions. A few paces to the right, she spied another door with a handle that she could pull. Traces of light gleamed from the edges, and she wondered where the passageway ended. It was a risk to open the door, especially with so many people in the castle, but she couldn't resist the urge.

To her surprise, she saw that she was in the library. And on the other side of the room, she saw Devon standing beside a bookcase.

She must have made a slight noise, for he turned to see her. Jane stepped back into the shadows, and he moved across the room, entering the passageway.

He closed the door behind him, and the faint light of the candle illuminated the space. "I think there is a matchmaking ghost in this castle. I had intended to join the others at dinner, but I kept feeling cold air around my shoulders and neck. It was unbearable, and it only went away when I left the dining room and came here."

His gaze passed over her white nightgown, and she saw his eyes darken with interest. "Should I leave you, Jane?"

She didn't want that at all. His very presence made her imagine all the things she had dreamed of earlier. And the need to be in his arms, to feel his kiss upon her mouth, was stronger than any common sense.

She moved to him and wrapped her arms around his neck. It was the only invitation he needed.

CHAPTER FIVE

In the dark space, no one knew they were here. There was no risk of discovery, and Jane gloried in the sensation when his mouth came down upon hers. His kiss was demanding, reckless in the way he possessed her. She kissed him back with all the fervor in her heart, surrendering to the needs rising within.

"My God, you smell good," he breathed, lowering his face to her throat. The scent of jasmine seemed to fill the air, and she gripped his hair, wanting so much more.

Devon never stopped touching her, and she felt his hands move down her back to her hips. Beneath the nightgown, she wore nothing at all. She knew she ought to feel ashamed of this, but nothing could have stopped her from being with this man.

Whether it was the herbs within the soap or an enchantment of some kind, she didn't know. But she loosened the ties of the nightgown, drawing his hand below the fabric. Only his touch seemed to ease the desire, and she needed him desperately.

Her body was so deeply aroused, she couldn't help but moan as he kissed her bare shoulder, his mouth moving lower. Her nightgown was falling against one shoulder, and he drew her hips to his. Against the juncture of her thighs, she felt his heated erection, and she wrapped one leg around his waist, not even knowing why.

He paused a moment, and then lifted her up. Her nightgown was tangled, but he pressed her against the back wall, guiding her other leg around his waist. He kissed her hard, claiming her mouth and her tongue, until she could hardly grasp a coherent thought. There was only this man and the arousal coursing inside her.

"I'm sorry," she murmured. "I don't know what's gotten into me. But I just…needed you so much. Bronson could have killed me today, and I cannot stop thinking of it."

"I wasn't going to let that happen. No matter what."

"I knew that, once you arrived. But after Marjorie left to get help, I was terrified that I would die alone." She kissed him again, offering him the taste of her lips.

He took from her, answering with his own mouth. When he trailed his lips over her throat, she felt a thousand shivers cross over her, as if her skin were opening beneath him.

"You're safe with me," he murmured. "I promise you."

But the words and the kisses weren't enough. Instead, it felt as if dormant needs had flared to life. She was falling in love with this man, and she wanted so much more.

Voices of warning started to intrude, but she shoved them back. Right now, she was in the arms of Devon Lancaster, the man whose touch she craved.

He continued to kiss a path lower, edging the upper swell of her breasts. For a moment, he paused, and she felt her body's disappointment. She touched his hair, guiding him lower, until his mouth covered her erect nipple.

The blast of heat roared through her as he licked the edge, gently suckling the tip. The pulling sensation made her moan, and she felt him adjusting her nightgown, freeing her from the twisted fabric.

"Don't stop," she breathed, arching as he sucked hard. Shimmering sensations flooded through her, and she was dimly aware that she was wet between her legs. To her shock, he pressed her back against the wall, moving his fingers between her thighs. She let out a mewling cry, and he began to stroke her intimately.

The wild feelings grew hotter, and she could hardly bear the sensations. This man's wicked touch was pulling apart her inhibitions until her breathing was coming in quick gasps. He slid a single finger inside and sucked against her nipple gently biting the tip as he caressed her.

"Devon," she pleaded, her voice hardly more than a whisper.

And then, he slid another finger inside. She was so wet, it didn't hurt at all. Instead, he seemed to reach inside her, finding every secret desire she'd ever held. He knew how to touch her, how to thrust his fingers as his mouth stimulated her. In the darkness, she lost all control, giving herself over to the pleasure of his touch.

He was murmuring endearments against her flesh, telling her how much he desired her. "Let yourself go, Jane. Trust that I will hold you."

He quickened the pace, his hand stroking and plunging, while his mouth claimed hers once again. She was straining hard, wanting him so badly.

And then, it seemed as if her body metamorphosed, unfolding as a shudder of sensation rocked through her. She let out a gasp, shaking as the climax rolled over her, her body shattering as his fingers remained buried inside.

Gently, he lowered her to stand, and her knees buckled. "Help me back to my room," she bade him.

Devon reached for the chamberstick with the fading candle and then walked with her back up the stairs. He pulled the door handle and held it so she could enter her bedroom.

For a moment, she stood beside him, feeling like the melted candle wax. He was going to let her go, but that wasn't what she wanted.

No longer did she feel like herself. It was as if the soap contained herbs that deepened every sensation of touch. And if he left her now, she would regret it for the rest of her life.

Gently, she led him into her room, pulling the secret door shut until it gave a slight click. Devon stood for a moment, his expression heated. "If I don't go back, Jane, I am never leaving your side. Not tonight. Not ever."

The weight of his words broke through to her. She knew he needed an heiress to marry, and her father's inheritance might provide that. But then again, there was no way of knowing how much she would receive.

Did she want to marry this man? Did she want to spend her days and nights with him at her side?

The answer was yes. She could not imagine anyone else. Silently, she moved to the door on the opposite side of the room. He followed her there and was about to turn the knob, when she reached out and turned the key in the lock.

His hand froze in place, and he stared at her. "Is this what you want?"

Never in his life had Devon felt so aroused by a woman. It was as if Jane had stolen away a piece of his soul. She stepped away from the door and pulled the pins from her hair. It fell around her shoulders in a light brown veil that hung to the middle of her back. There was a slight curl to it, and he reached out to touch a few strands.

Her face was pale but she took his hands and guided them to her loose nightgown. Holding his hands, she helped him push back the fabric until it pooled on the floor, leaving her naked body exposed.

The scent of her skin was driving him to madness. The aroma of jasmine filled his senses until he was aware of nothing else. He lifted her into his arms and brought her back to the bed. By locking the door, she had given her consent.

He knew that he ought to stop her now, to leave and let her remain untouched. But her ardent response in the passageway had driven him past the brink. He intended to marry this woman, and devil that he was, he would never turn away from her offering.

Her body was slender, with full breasts and nipples the color of a spring rose. Her waist dipped before it swelled to hips and a curved bottom that was made for his hands. He needed to taste every inch of her, and he wanted to slide his erection deep into her wet entrance.

Devon brought her to the bed, laying her down before sitting beside her. He removed his jacket and waistcoat, untying his cravat and pulling his shirt off. Jane reached up to trace his bare skin, her palms moving over his chest.

"You're strong," she said softly. Her fingers outlined his pectoral muscles, and he felt his heart pounding with need. Though he supposed she might be frightened of seeing him fully naked, he was beyond all control. He stripped his breeches and the remainder of his clothes until he was naked. Then he moved atop her, keeping his weight on his forearms.

Jane smiled at him, and in her blue eyes, he saw trust and desire. She moved her hands down his back to his hips, shifting her body against him so that his manhood thrust between them. The motion made him grit his teeth, for he was stone hard right now. It was all he could do not to lift her knees and sink deep inside her.

Instead, he turned his attention toward worshipping her body. He kissed a path down to her breasts, flicking his tongue against her nipple until her hands fisted the coverlet. With his hands, he took her hips and tilted them up, sliding his palms over the curve of her bottom. She parted her legs, and he saw the glistening pearl of her.

"I'm not going to stop touching you," he warned. "I'm going to fill your body and join with you until you cannot feel anything but me."

Jane didn't doubt that she was caught beneath a spell of some kind. This man held her in his thrall, and when he bent his mouth to taste her intimately, she bit back a scream. He was gentle, teasing her hooded flesh with his tongue, and he guided her legs over his shoulders. Sensations coursed through her, and she felt her body coming apart. "Devon, I d-don't know if I can bear this." She was shaking now, but he never stopped working her flesh with his tongue. The raw sensation overtook her, and she gasped as the flood of release crescendoed through her in a wave of pleasure.

He let her ride out the storm and then lowered her hips again. Between her legs, she felt the slight pressure of his manhood, and he slowly pressed against her wetness. They fit together easily, and even when he claimed her virginity, she felt almost no pain at all.

Devon moved slowly, gently sliding in and out. His

face held the tension of a man who was riding the edge of arousal. She moved in counterpoint to his thrusts, meeting him, and heard his swift exhale.

"Careful, Jane," he warned. "I'm trying to be gentle with you."

But she wanted to make him feel the same breathless release she'd been given. She squeezed her inner walls, feeling the pressure of his length, and was rewarded with his groan.

"Did that hurt you?"

"God, no. Do it again."

She obeyed, squeezing tightly as he entered and withdrew. His mouth came down over her nipple again, and the sensation only deepened the pleasure of having him plunge inside her. She gripped his hair, arching her back as she thrust back. He let out a growl and penetrated again, punishing her by sucking hard against her breast.

A bolt of heat shot through her, and she lost control of herself. She no longer cared about anything else, but instead, she wrapped her legs around him and encouraged him to move faster.

This time, he did, and she let him ride her hard, squeezing against his erection as he pumped inside her. She felt him straining, and he demanded, "I want to feel you come apart again. With me inside you."

It was strangely empowering to realize that he was not going to claim his own release until she did. She stared into his eyes, letting go of her body, and when he began quickening his pace, he seized her bottom and held her hard as he thrust. She felt the rise of her body, and shifted her legs again, raising higher until she felt him pressing against a sensitive place.

He sensed what she wanted and continued to hold her while he penetrated her, stroking her on the inside.

The tide of need swept her under again, and she convulsed beneath him, feeling him grind against her until her body quaked and she trembled with the force of her release. His handsome face was grim, continuing to pump inside her until her tremors stilled. Only then did he spill himself within her.

Her body jerked with a few aftershocks, but she kept her legs wrapped around him, needing his body upon hers. He remained inside her, and she tried not to let herself worry. He had promised that he would never leave her. And though she had let him seduce her—or perhaps she had seduced him—she told herself that she was not at all like her mother.

Everything would be different with Devon. He'd said so, hadn't he?

But even with their bodies joined together, she couldn't help but worry that she had made a grave mistake.

Devon knew that others were going to come looking for Jane. At the very least, a maid would intrude, and he could not allow her to be embarrassed like that. For a while, he let her sleep, tracing the outline of her sleeping form. She was resting peacefully, and yet, this day could have ended in tragedy.

Although Lord Banfield had ensured that Bronson was taken into custody, Devon couldn't let go of his protective instincts. This woman had threaded her way into his heart, and he hardly cared if she was an heiress or not. She was both vulnerable and brave in the face of danger. He could never imagine walking away from her, nor did he want to.

But at this moment, it was too dangerous to remain in her bed.

He brushed a soft kiss against her shoulder, coaxing her to roll over. Then he took her in a kiss, aware of when her drowsiness faded and she grew conscious of what they had done.

In her eyes, he saw the worry, though she rested one hand against his shoulder. "Don't be afraid," he said quietly. "It was never my intent for it to go this far. But I do want to marry you, Jane."

The tension only heightened, instead of joy. "And what if you find out that I am not an heiress? What if my inheritance is only a handful of pounds?"

He had already considered this. "It doesn't matter. We will find a way to get by."

Her blue eyes grew uncertain. "Your father may not give permission for you to wed me. If he learns you have offered for a vicar's daughter—"

"An earl's daughter," he corrected.

"His by-blow, you mean." Jane pulled back from him, drawing the covers over her body. She closed her eyes a moment, and admitted, "They will not support a marriage between us."

"I do not require my father's permission to wed, and you are also of age to marry." He recognized her fears and added, "You don't have to worry about me leaving you, Jane. I know that I want you."

She sat up, still clutching the bedclothes to her body. "You say that now. But if I drive a wedge between you and your family, you will come to resent me. I don't know what I was thinking, letting this happen." Her voice dropped to a whisper. "I let myself fall beneath your spell, believing in stories. But we are from two different worlds."

"Don't," he warned. Devon sat up and took her hands in his, kissing her again. "You're allowing fear to rule your head. I want to marry you. The only question you should ask yourself is if you want to wed me." He stroked her fingers, bringing them to rest on his shoulders.

"I couldn't bear it if you grew to hate me," she said.

Before he could answer, a knock sounded at the door. "Jane? It's Marjorie. May I come in?" The doorknob turned, and Devon muttered a curse.

"Just a moment," Jane said.

Devon nodded toward the passage way, telling her without words that he had to leave. He handed Jane her nightgown, swiftly pulling on his clothing as fast as he could. With his clothing unbuttoned, he took his shoes and darted into the passageway, closing the door behind him.

He should have left, but instead, he heard Jane unlock her room and allow Marjorie to enter.

"I came to see if you were all right," Marjorie began. A moment later, she said, "You look dreadful. Your mouth is swollen, and your hair is everywhere."

Devon smiled in the darkness, knowing exactly why Jane appeared so bedraggled. He adjusted his clothing, fumbling with the buttonholes in the dark. But he was unprepared when he heard Jane burst into tears.

"I'm not all right, Marjorie," she sobbed. "I'm not."

He froze in place and heard the young woman offer comforting sounds. "There, there. Of course you're not. That horrible man tried to kill you, and I was practically useless to help you."

But Devon pressed his hand against the cool wall, realizing that Jane was not crying about the danger. She was weeping out of regret.

He let out a slow sigh, realizing the extent of what he'd done. Jane had come to him, and he'd taken advantage of her innocence, seducing her thoroughly. And now that she was ruined, no doubt she feared she would become the same as her mother.

He would never let that happen. But it did seem that she had become a reluctant bride, not believing that he would follow through on his word.

Devon finished dressing in the dark, determined to prove her wrong. She didn't believe she was the woman he wanted to spend the rest of his life with. And how could she believe it, when they had known each other a matter of days?

Yet, with her, he felt the loneliness fade away. When they had spent the time stranded in the wine cellar together, he was startled to realize that he'd enjoyed being with her. He'd played cards and danced in the library with her, savoring every moment. Why wouldn't he want to spend months and years at her side?

Marjorie's voice drew his attention, and he overheard her say, "Don't worry about anything, Jane. I promise you, it will be all right."

It would be, he vowed to himself. And he intended to speak with Lord Banfield, to ask permission to marry her.

But first, there were some things he needed to do.

CHAPTER SIX

ONE DAY LATER

"You do not have my permission wed Miss Hawkins," Lord Banfield said. The earl sat back in a chair, behaving as if Devon were discussing the weather. "I fear you have been misled by Mr. Hunt."

Misled? What was the man talking about?

"I don't understand." Devon took a seat opposite the earl. He had spent all of yesterday trying to get an engagement ring for Jane to properly propose to her. Some of his friends had insisted that he pay a visit to the gypsies with them, and he'd gone along. Although he had tried to see Jane during the trip, Lady Marjorie had practically pinned herself to Jane's side. There was never any moment to get her alone.

The earl cleared his throat. "Mr. Hunt made it seem as if Jane was to receive a large inheritance from the late Lord Banfield. I understand you learned the truth, that she was his illegitimate daughter. But since we have recently learned that Lady Banfield is not, in fact, dead, the portion Jane was meant to receive may not be hers anymore. It would likely be part of Lady Banfield's dower property."

Devon stared at the earl and realized that Bronson had known all along that Lady Banfield was still alive. The footman had been desperate to keep her from learning about Jane, and his own madness had nearly cost Jane her life.

"Was it Lady Banfield that Jane heard screaming that day?"

"It must have been," the earl agreed. He shook his head and shrugged. "I don't understand why the servants tried to keep it a secret. It might be they were afraid she would leave her rooms and try to hurt the guests. Or even herself, in a fit of madness."

"And Bronson was trying to protect her."

The earl nodded. "Indeed."

"Then why did Mr. Hunt say nothing to you? Didn't he know that the dowager countess was still alive?"

"He did. But he was ordered to say nothing until the will reading. The late earl did not want anyone to know of his wife's madness." Lord Banfield folded his arms across his chest. "I am sorry if this alters your plans, but you must not rely upon any sort of inheritance from Jane. She is the adopted daughter of a vicar, and that is all."

Instead of feeling disappointment, Devon wasn't at all deterred. "I need to speak with her."

"I am certain you do. But I ask you to be aware that Jane has a tender heart. She does not deserve to be cast aside as her mother was."

Devon stood and faced the earl. "Lord Banfield, I apologize if you believed I had less than honorable intentions toward Miss Hawkins. I know she is like another daughter to you."

"She is. And for that reason, I will not let any man

break her heart. Especially a man whose only interest is in an inheritance."

Devon stiffened at the accusation. Though he supposed the earl had every reason to believe this, it wasn't true at all. "I asked your permission because her adopted father, the vicar, is not here. But even without your approval, I intend to ask her to wed me." It felt like the right decision, and in this, he would not waver.

"Even if she inherits nothing but a few pounds?" the earl asked.

"Even then." Devon gave the man a nod of acknowledgment. "Now, if you will excuse me, I need to find Miss Hawkins."

"She was walking in the gardens with Marjorie, so I heard." The earl's expression warmed, and he added, "I am glad to hear that you have not changed your mind, despite her penniless state. Jane deserves to be happy."

"If she will marry me, I vow that she will be."

Jane walked through the gardens with Marjorie, feeling like a prisoner while her best friend never stopped talking. She had confided her secret, needing to share her dilemma, and the young woman had sworn not to tell anyone. Even so, she had promised that she would protect Jane—no matter what happened.

They had reached the steps leading back to the house when a sudden gust of frigid air whipped at her shawl. Jane tried to catch it, but the wind drew it out of her grasp.

It landed at the feet of Devon Lancaster. He picked it up and held it out, smiling at her. "Would you take a walk with me, Miss Hawkins?"

Her heart pounded at the sight of him. She had seen

him briefly when they had traveled with the others to the gypsy camp, but Marjorie had refused to let her speak to him then. Now, she realized that even a single day apart had made her miss him more.

But Marjorie had other ideas. "She would rather walk with the devil than walk with you," her friend shot back.

"Some have called me that," Devon admitted. But he extended his arm and asked, "May I speak with you alone, Miss Hawkins?"

Her face was troubled, and she glanced at Marjorie. Her friend shook her head. "Absolutely not. Jane and I were—" Her words were cut off when a gust of air shoved her sideways. Marjorie yelped, and Jane was stunned to see the Tudor ghost beaming with mischief.

"Marjorie, I think you'd better go. I will be fine."

And protected by a ghost, no less. From the look on Devon's face, he, too, had seen the spirit.

"I don't think it's a good idea." Her friend started to walk toward them, but the wind picked up again, blowing her bonnet toward the door.

"Only for a moment," Jane insisted. And with any luck, the ghost would leave her friend alone. She sent him a pointed look, but the bearded ghost smiled.

Jane adjusted her shawl and put her hand in the crook of Devon's arm. He led her toward the arbor, which was covered in climbing pink roses. When they were out of earshot, she whispered, "Did you see the…ghost?"

"I did. He is Benedict, and I must confess I asked him for his help with Marjorie. I wanted to speak to you yesterday, but she was rather adamant about protecting you. I needed spiritual intervention today."

"She is my dearest friend," Jane said. And after she'd confessed her ruin, Marjorie would have battled an army of ghosts to help her.

Devon drew her to sit upon a stone bench beside the hedge maze. "I spoke with Lord Banfield this morning, and he did not grant me permission to marry you."

Her heart pounded with a sudden burst of anxiety. It seemed as if the blood had stopped flowing from her heart, and a numbness settled over her. Did this mean he was giving up on her?

"I also learned that there is no ghost in the turret. Lady Banfield was the one screaming, and it alters the will. Only a few people had any idea she was still alive, though Lady Banfield is...incapable of being mistress of Castle Keyvnor." He had turned serious now, and she lowered her gaze. She didn't want to hear his next words, and she had a feeling that the worst had come to pass. Her inheritance was worth nothing at all, and he was going to leave her.

A ringing noise sounded in her ears, and she felt faint. Her hands were freezing, and when he took her palm in his, she hardly felt anything at all.

"I know what this means," she whispered.

"Do you?" His voice held kindness, and the last thing she wanted was to see pity in his eyes. "Look at me, Jane."

She hesitated, but a petal blew into her face. The breeze swelled, and before she knew what was happening, more rose petals drifted around her. She finally lifted her gaze to Devon's and it seemed that a thousand flowers were filling up the air, like snowflakes. The soft aroma of roses surrounded her, and the sight filled her with wonder. She also heard the sound of lute music, and noticed Benedict standing nearby, playing a song for them.

"Will you do me the honor of becoming my wife?" Devon asked. From his waistcoat pocket, he withdrew a small gold ring with a ruby and two smaller diamonds.

The gold was engraved in a twisting band, and he slid it on her finger.

She stared at it in disbelief, hardly able to speak. When she did open her mouth, a flower petal stuck to her lips.

At that, she began to laugh. The Tudor ghost continued to play, and she nearly got a mouthful of flowers. "I cannot answer because there are roses everywhere."

The ghost waved his hand and the flower petals drifted to the ground. Devon brushed the flowers away from her face, and she took his hand. "Are you certain this is what you want, Devon? I may not have anything at all, once the will is read. I don't ever want to come between you and your family."

"You will not. But I need you with me, Jane." He stroked her hair, cupping her face. "If I have to gain the help of a hundred ghosts to make you marry me, I will ask it." His thumb brushed over her lips, and this time, her quickening pulse had nothing to do with fear—and everything to do with joy.

"I want to love you, Jane. For each day of the rest of my life, if you will have me."

She felt the answering love in her own heart, for this man who had stood by her in danger. "I would like that, Devon." As soon as she spoke the words, there were no doubts in her mind. This man had never made her feel like less of a woman. He had made her feel more, like a helpmate and a partner who would stand by him always.

He drew her closer into a more lingering kiss. Above them, the sun shone brightly, and the sound of lute music echoed in the wind.

And when she drew back from his embrace, more flower petals drifted toward them. She laughed and turned back to the ghost. "You had better stop, Benedict, or there will be no flowers left."

The ghost smiled broadly, and she thought she heard the rumbling of laughter before he disappeared into the sunlight.

Epilogue

Mr. Hunt cleared his voice and read from the will. "To Jane Hawkins, Lord Banfield bequeaths the estate of Kirkbourne. He regrets that he could never acknowledge you as his daughter, but he hopes that the land will compensate for his indiscretion."

Jane blinked a moment, unable to believe what she had just heard. "An estate?" She stared at Devon as if surely she had misheard the bequest.

Devon took Jane's hand in his while Mr. Hunt finished reading Lord Banfield's will. In a low voice he murmured in her ear. "I am happy for you, Jane. But know that it doesn't matter to me; I would marry you if you had nothing at all."

Jane's hand clenched his, until her engagement ring dug into his flesh. He had never seen her this agitated before. In a hushed whisper, she insisted, "But Lord Banfield said I would inherit very little, since Lady Banfield is still alive."

"He wanted us to believe that because he feared I was a fortune hunter. But Lady Banfield already had her dower portion and yours was protected. Only Lord Banfield and Mr. Hunt knew about it." He caressed her knuckles. "I think he was being protective for your sake, Jane. No one else knew, save Mr. Hunt."

"I can't breathe." She sat down, fanning herself. "I feel as if I've just inherited a kingdom."

Devon didn't tell her that it might as well be that. The Kirkbourne estate had over a thousand acres, and there were sheep, horses, and even mines along the coast. It lay near Bideford, and Jane would never need to worry about money for the rest of her life. It was large enough to bring her adopted parents, the Engelmeyers, to live there, which was important to her. He had already made the decision to settle in Kirkbourne, and he would visit his own property from time to time, leaving it in the hands of his land steward to manage.

"I am happy for you," he murmured. "And I think this was your father's way of atoning for what he did."

She squeezed his hand, and her engagement ring gleamed in the light. "I suppose. But I am sorry that my birth had to cause so much sorrow for anyone." Lady Banfield had learned of her existence and had gone silent for days within the turret.

"You are not at fault," Devon whispered. "And I, for one, am very glad of your birth. Whether you were born of a vicar or an earl." He traced the edge of her ring with his thumb. "I love you, Jane Hawkins."

"And I love you." She smiled at him, covering his hand with her own.

Devon leaned in to whisper. "Will you dance with me in the library later?"

"Later," she promised with a secretive smile. "And every night, for the rest of our lives."

Don't forget to claim your FREE e-book
by Michelle Willingham!

Visit http://www.michellewillingham.com/contact/
for more information.

If you enjoyed "A Dance with the Devil,"
here's an excerpt from Michelle's newest book.

GOOD EARLS DON'T LIE

CHAPTER ONE

YORKSHIRE
MAY 1846

His head was killing him. It felt as if a hundred horses had trampled his skull, and right now he tasted blood and dirt in his mouth. After a moment, Iain Donovan gathered his senses, clearing his head.

The last thing he remembered was riding toward the Penford estate. He dimly recalled having passed a grove of trees when, abruptly, he'd been knocked off his horse. A shattering pain had crashed over him, and he vaguely remembered voices arguing and shouting.

But no one was here now.

Iain tried to sit up, and blood rushed to his head, threatening a loss of consciousness once again. He reached out to touch his brother's signet ring, only to find it gone. A sense of fear rose up in him, and he uttered a foul curse.

No one knew him here. He'd never left Ireland before now, and this country was completely foreign to him. While his mother had taken his older brother Michael to

London every Season, teaching him all the skills necessary to become the Earl of Ashton, Iain had been left at home. She had done everything in her power to ensure that he was the invisible spare, the hidden son of no importance.

None of that mattered now. He was the only heir left, and he intended to prove that he was a man of worth. He would rebuild Ashton and help his people—even if that meant traveling across the Irish Sea to meet with strangers.

The wind sent gooseflesh rising over his skin, and when he realized he was no longer wearing a shirt, he let out another curse. Who would do such a thing? The bloody bastards had seized the shirt off his back, devil take them all and eat them sideways.

The thieves had stolen not only the ring and the few coins he possessed, but his horse, his coat, waistcoat, and shirt—even the shoes he'd worn. A fine welcome to England this was. After leaving the nightmare of Ireland behind him, he'd thought that here, everything would be better.

Apparently not.

Iain rose to his feet and studied the land around him. It was a fair day, with the sun shining over rolling hills and meadows. He supposed he could walk the remaining distance to the Penford estate, for it was only a few miles farther. Though he didn't particularly like the idea of walking in his trousers and stocking feet, he had no other choice.

He grimaced as he followed the road leading toward Penford. All the baggage he'd brought from Ashton was gone now. He'd have to borrow clothes and shoes, and no one would possibly believe he was the Earl of Ashton. Without a coach, servants, clothing, or a signet ring, they'd think him a beggar at best.

His head was pounding from the mild wound, but more than the physical pain was a rising sense of panic.

Calm down, he ordered himself. He would tell the truth about his ill luck, and surely someone would believe him. Lady Wolcroft had visited Ashton a few years ago. Surely she would remember him. After all, she was the one who had invited him to visit when she'd learned of the troubles they had suffered with the famine. His mother, Moira, and Lady Wolcroft's daughter, Iris, had been good friends at boarding school. Moira had spent all her school holidays with Iris's family and was like another daughter to them.

But friendship aside, he couldn't suppress the rise of uneasiness. Aside from Lady Wolcroft and his tenants, very few outsiders even knew there *was* a spare, in addition to the heir. His gut twisted at his mother's disregard, but he pushed the anger back.

Despite the circumstances, his younger sisters were depending on him to save their estate. For Colleen and Sybil, he would not fail. *Could* not fail. The task before him was greater than any he'd ever imagined, but he was determined to prove his mother wrong and restore Ashton to its former wealth.

And so it was that Iain had decided to travel across the sea, to leave his familiar homeland and dwell among strangers. And most of all, to offer himself up in marriage, in the hopes of wooing a wealthy bride.

Most men would never dream of such a thing, but his pride had crumbled as surely as the estate of Ashton. His brother was dead, and his sisters needed him. He'd be damned if he'd turn his back on them, forcing them to wed strangers. No. There was a way out of this mess, even if it meant offering himself up as the sacrificial lamb.

With each step, Iain gathered command of himself

until he was confident that he *would* be welcomed at Penford, despite his bedraggled appearance.

As he continued along the dry road leading toward the hills, he saw sprouts of barley and rye emerging from the soil. The sight was a sobering contrast to the rotting fields he'd left behind at Ashton. The blight had destroyed their potato crops, until there was naught left, save a crumbling castle and enough debts to bury the family alive.

His mother and sisters had gone to stay with their aunt in New York, while he managed the affairs at Ashton. He had no intention of abandoning the estate or the people who had called it home for all their lives.

For they were starving. Too many of them had watched their crops rot in the earth, and they had nothing left. No livestock, no money—nothing to trade for food. Hundreds had left in the hopes of finding work elsewhere, but no one wanted Irish refugees.

Iain knew that if he wed an heiress, his bride's dowry could help the tenants survive until the crops improved. And though he had little to offer, save his Irish charm and a decrepit castle, he had to try.

The road curved over a hill, and when he crossed the apex, he saw Penford within the valley. On the west side of the estate, he spied a lake, gleaming silver and gold in the morning sunlight. For a moment, he paused to enjoy the sight. The estate was near a village, though it lay in an isolated part of Yorkshire—not exactly the best place to find a wife.

But Lady Wolcroft had her own motives for bringing him here...and he would do anything necessary to form an alliance with the matron. She could bring him into her circles in London, introducing Iain to potential brides—and he was well aware that she had her own unmarried granddaughters. He would certainly consider the young ladies as marriage prospects before he left for London.

He continued the painful walk down the road, and when he turned the corner, he spied two adolescent boys on horseback. On *his* horse, Darcy.

Damn them all and may the crows feast upon their bones.

Iain didn't call out to them, for they could easily outpace him. Instead, he began running lightly, hoping he could overtake them before they noticed his arrival. The rocks dug into the soles of his feet as he ran hard, and he bit back the pain. Almost there…

"The horse is mine," one of the boys insisted. "I found him first."

"No, he's mine," the other boy glared. "I'm going to tell Father that he followed me home."

They couldn't have been more than thirteen, he guessed. Their thievery was likely adolescent mischief, and he fully intended to get every last one of his possessions back. He quickened his pace, but within seconds, Darcy grew skittish and neighed, alerting the boys to his presence.

At that, Iain shouted out, "Stop, both of you! That's my horse!"

"I told you we shouldn't have done it!" one cried out, urging Darcy faster. "Go!"

His idiot horse obeyed the command and galloped hard until there was no hope of catching up to them. Iain ran as fast as he could, hoping to glimpse where they were going, but the boys disappeared into the trees.

He cursed beneath his breath, furious at the way this day had begun. It was bad enough to be robbed, much less by boys. But it wouldn't take long to identify them to the authorities.

His feet were bleeding through his stockings, and his

body was perspiring from the hard run. A sight he would be, arriving at Penford like this. He'd have to improve his appearance before arriving, or else they'd toss him back into the road like yesterday's breakfast.

Iain walked the remaining distance to the manor house, keeping off the gravel road. Several of the tenants eyed him as he passed, but he kept walking, his shoulders held back as if it were the most normal thing in the world to arrive at an estate wearing only trousers.

Tall hedges stood beside the house, and a small arbor led into a garden. He hurried toward it, feeling sheepish about his lack of attire. It might be that he could find a footman or a gardener who could help him with clothing. But as he approached the garden, he realized that he had entered a maze of hedges. Curiosity got the better of him, and he began wandering through the boxwood aisles.

At one end, he saw a stone fountain with rosebushes planted beside it. Deeper within the maze, he found a bed of irises, their purple blossoms illuminated by the sun. And when he reached the farthest end, he saw lilies of the valley.

He stood for a moment at the edge of the maze, where it opened onto a green lawn. A lovely woman was seated upon a stone bench, a book lying beside her. Her hair was reddish brown, tucked into a neat updo beneath her bonnet. She closed her eyes for a moment, lifting her face toward the sun like a blossom.

The sight of her stole the words from his brain, and Iain decided that his missing horse could wait, for the time being.

Who was this woman? One of Lady Wolcroft's granddaughters? It was possible, given her white morning gown trimmed with blue embroidery. Every inch of her appeared to be a lady. Iain took a few steps closer, fascinated by her.

The young woman dug her fingers into the stone bench, and her face tightened. Slowly, she eased herself to the edge of the seat, and she hunched her back. She gripped the bench hard, as if every movement was a struggle. Iain tensed, trying to understand her difficulty. It was only a moment later when he realized what she was doing.

She was trying to stand up.

The woman leaned heavily against the bench as she tried to force her legs to bear weight. When her knees buckled, she sat down again, her spirits dismayed.

Iain let out the breath he'd been holding. The pieces were beginning to fall into place. It might be that Lady Wolcroft had asked him here to help her granddaughters. If this young woman couldn't walk, there was no chance of her finding a husband.

And yet, she had a courage that he admired. There was a quiet determination in her eyes, of a woman who would not give up. He understood her.

Softly, he emerged from the hedgerow, wanting to know who she was.

There was a strange man standing in her garden.

Lady Rose Thornton blinked a moment, wondering if her imagination had conjured him. Because he was also half-naked and smiling at her, as if nothing were the matter.

"You'll have to forgive me for being half-clothed, *a chara*," he apologized, "but I was robbed on my journey here by a group of damned thieving boys."

Now what did he mean by that? Rose shut her eyes

tightly and opened them again. No, he was still there. She filled her lungs with air, prepared to scream for all that was holy.

"I won't be harming you," he said, lifting his hands in surrender, "but I would be most grateful for some clothes. Not yours, of course." He sent her a roguish grin.

She gaped at him, still uncertain of who he was. But she had to admit that he *was* indeed an attractive man, in a pirate sort of way. His brown hair was cut short, and his cheeks were bristled, as if he'd forgotten to shave. She tried not to stare at his bare chest, but he cocked his head and rested his hands at his waist. His chest muscles were well defined, his skin tawny from the sun. Ridges at his abdomen caught her eye, and it was clear enough that he was a working man. Perhaps a groom or a footman. Gentlemen did not possess muscles like these, especially if they lived a life of leisure. His green eyes were staring at her with amusement, and Rose found herself spellbound by his presence.

"Do you not speak," he asked, "or have I cast you into silence with my nakedness?"

"Y-you're not naked," she blurted out. Her anxiety twisted up inside her, and she began babbling. "That is, you're mostly covered," she corrected, her face flaming. "The important bits, anyway."

Not naked? What sort of remark was that? She was sitting in the garden with a stranger wearing only trousers, and she hadn't yet called out for help. What was the matter with her? He could be an intruder bent upon attacking her.

But he laughed at her remark. It was a rich, deep tone that reminded her of wickedness.

Rose couldn't help but wonder why on earth a footman was naked in her garden. "Stay back," she warned, "or I'll scream."

He lifted his hands. "You needn't do that. As I've said, I have no intention of harming you. I fear you've caught me in a kettle of pottage. Could you be helping me, if it's not too much trouble?" With a slight lift of an eyebrow, he added, "I am here at Lady Wolcroft's invitation."

That nudged her curiosity. Why would her grandmother summon a stranger to Penford? Mildred loved nothing better than to meddle, but she wasn't even here at the moment. She had gone to Bath only a few weeks ago.

Then again, it was entirely possible that this man was lying. Probable, even.

"Who are you?" she managed to ask. "And why are you here?"

"I am Iain Donovan, the Earl of Ashton," he answered. "At your service." He bowed, and in his grin, she detected a teasing air. An Irishman, she was certain, given his speech patterns. But an earl? Exactly how empty headed did he think she was?

Rose folded her hands in her lap. "There is no need to lie, sir," she told him. "I know full well that you are not an earl."

He blinked at that, his face furrowed. But honestly, had he really thought he could pull off such a deception? She was no country miss, easily fooled. "An earl would travel in a coach with dozens of servants. Never alone."

Before he could argue with her, she continued. "You may go to the servants' entrance, and our housekeeper, Mrs. Marlock, might have some old clothes to lend you. Perhaps a bit of food, and you can be on your way." Though she kept her tone reasonable, she had no way of knowing whether this man was dangerous. Perhaps she should have screamed after all. There was still time to do so.

The man crossed his arms over his chest and regarded her. In an even tone, he said, "I've not spoken any lies, miss."

"It's Lady Rose, Mr. Donovan," she corrected. As far as she was concerned, this man was a commoner with no claim to any title. "I should like for you to leave. Now." Her nerves tightened, for if this man dared to threaten her, she could do nothing to stop him. Especially since she couldn't run.

Even if she did call out to her footman, Calvert, he might not arrive quickly enough. Her gaze seized upon a rake nearby, and she wondered if she could reach it, if the need arose.

"I've no reason to speak untruths," he said. "As I told you before, I was robbed on my way here." He paused a moment, adding, "The axle broke on our coach, and my servants stayed behind to fix it. I thought it best to continue on horseback, since Lady Wolcroft invited me to stay as her guest."

"An unlikely story," Rose countered. "If you really *were* the earl, you'd have brought several footmen with you."

He raised an eyebrow. "And how many footmen was I expected to have?"

"Enough to bring several of them with you. A gentleman never travels alone."

The man's expression turned thunderous. "He does, when there's no other choice." It looked like he was about to argue further, but instead, he tightened his mouth and said, "Lady Wolcroft's eldest daughter and my mother were friends. She wants to marry me off to an Englishwoman, and that is why I am here."

She didn't believe him one whit. No, he had to be a vagrant of some sort, a man down on his luck who was attempting to take advantage by lying. "Well, sir, you do spin an entertaining tale. I've heard that the Irish are excellent storytellers, but you can take your story back to our housekeeper."

"It's not a story, Lady Rose. I *am* here to find a bride." The intensity in his voice was rather strong, and made no secret of his annoyance.

She leaned as far over as she dared and managed to reach the rake handle. It made her feel better having a makeshift weapon.

"What are you planning to do with that rake, *a chara*?" he inquired, taking another step closer. Rose gripped the handle with both hands and drew it closer, using the tool to keep him at a distance.

"Nothing, if you go away." Truthfully, she didn't know exactly what she would do with the rake. It wasn't exactly suitable for stabbing someone. She could poke him with it, but not much else.

This time, she did call out to her footman. "Calvert! I have need of your assistance!" She hoped he would guard her against any threat. Right now, she wanted the strange man gone from her presence.

Even if he was quite handsome. And a charming liar.

The Irishman's mouth twisted, and he bowed. "As you like, then, Lady Rose. I'll be seeing you later, when I've better clothes to wear than these."

She wasn't certain what to think of that, but she gripped the rake tightly. "Be on your way." *Or I'll have my footman remove you.*

But as the stranger disappeared into the maze, she was aware that her heart was beating swiftly, out of more than fear. Although she had seen her brother without a shirt before, never had she seen a man like Iain Donovan. His dark hair had a hint of curl to it, and those green eyes fascinated her. His cheekbones were sharp, his face lean and chiseled. He looked like a man who had walked through hell itself and come out stronger.

There was nothing at all refined about him. She'd wager that he'd never worn gloves in his life.

No. He could not possibly be an earl.

And yet...she'd been intrigued by his physical strength, wondering if his muscles were as firm as they appeared. His form could have been carved out of marble, like a statue.

When Calvert arrived upon the path to take her back to the house, she stole a look back at the maze. As soon as she was safely inside, she intended for her footman to follow Mr. Donovan and find out the real reason why he was here.

"Well, now, I don't know as I'm believing ye, lad." Mrs. Marlock planted her hands upon her broad waist. "Lady Wolcroft said naught about a houseguest arriving from Ireland. But if'n I'm wrong, I'd be a fair sight embarrassed to turn ye out again. I suppose ye mun have some clothes, aye?"

"Aye, that is true enough." Iain was well aware of his impoverished appearance, but there was naught to be done about it. "If I could speak with Lady Wolcroft, I'm certain she will sort it all out."

Mrs. Marlock tilted her head to the side as if assessing his story. Her gray hair was bound and pinned up beneath a cap. She reminded him of a soldier, though she had a ring of house keys instead of a sword at her plump waist. "Lady Wolcroft isn't here, and I can't be certain when she'll return from Bath."

Bath? Why had she gone there after she'd invited him to come visit? Well, now this was a fine kettle of fish.

He had no clothes, no money, no signet ring, and no one to welcome him to Penford.

The housekeeper continued, "Have ye any other proof of who ye are?"

No, he had nothing at all. He'd been stripped of everything, may the thieves be eaten in tiny pieces, bite by bite. Iain's frustration rose up, but he forced himself to tamp it down. The last thing he needed was to frighten the housekeeper.

He searched for a believable lie. "My servants will be arriving today with my belongings, once my coach is repaired," he said smoothly. "That should be all the proof you need." He spoke calmly, keeping his tone even so as not to intimidate Mrs. Marlock. If he gave her any reason to doubt him, she would throw him out.

He was on borrowed time, and he had no means of proving his identity. If Lady Wolcroft were here, there was some chance she might recognize him. But no one else would.

The housekeeper didn't appear convinced. "Ye say ye've come from Ireland, is that so?"

"I come from Ashton," he answered. "In County Mayo." For a moment, he waited to see if she had other questions. When she said nothing, he added, "I imagine Lady Wolcroft may have spoken of my mother, Moira, has she not? Or my brother, Michael, God rest him?"

Mrs. Marlock folded her arms and frowned. "Nay, she hasn't." She eyed him as if trying to make a decision. At last, she said, "Well, there could be some truth in what ye say, but until Lady Wolcroft returns, I can't be letting a stranger into the house. Ye can return in a few days, and see if she's back home again."

Her refusal didn't surprise him at all. But he didn't want to be turned out in the middle of Yorkshire with no shelter, no money, and no food. Thinking quickly, he decided upon an alternative. "I'll swear to you that I *am* the Earl of Ashton. Allow me to stay this night, and once my servants arrive at Penford, I should be glad to compensate you handsomely for the trouble." He wasn't quite certain how he'd manage it, but he would find a way.

The housekeeper only smiled. "And when the Queen arrives, she'll offer me proof that I'm her long-lost daughter." With a shake of her head, she added, "Nay, sir, ye'd best go now. I'm certain ye can find someone in the village who'll be giving ye a place to bide for a wee bit."

Iain highly doubted it, given his state of undress. No, it was far better to talk Mrs. Marlock into letting him remain at Penford. "And what if I offered to...that is—" He hesitated, wondering if it would hurt his cause to lower himself further.

What choice do you have? he thought to himself. *No one knows who you are.*

He bit back his pride and asked, "What if I gave you my assistance on the estate? At least until my servants can prove who I am." It was the best compromise he could give. He'd done his share of menial labor on Ashton, after most of the tenants had left or died. It had been unavoidable, and he would set aside his pride if it meant gaining shelter for the night.

Mrs. Marlock frowned, crossing her arms as she stared at him. "I already asked ye to leave, sir. Ye've no references, and despite yer manner of speech, ye're a stranger among us. There's no place for ye here."

Iain straightened and regarded her with all seriousness. "Mrs. Marlock, what will Lady Wolcroft say to you when she learns that you turned away her guest?"

The old woman hesitated, and her uncertainty made

him press further. "All I ask is to remain here for a single day. I need not stay in the main house, if it makes you uncomfortable."

She narrowed her gaze. "I don't know ye, sir. And it's our butler, Mr. Fulton, ye'll have to speak with. I cannot give ye a place to stay within this household. It's nae possible."

"A few hours, then," he bargained. "Just until my servants arrive."

Though he had no desire to sleep outside, if he couldn't convince Mrs. Marlock or Fulton that he was the earl, he'd have no choice. And while he might be a slightly adventurous sort, sleeping on the moors would be colder than the devil's conscience.

He sent her a warm smile, and added, "You do seem to be a charitable woman, Mrs. Marlock. I know you'd not ask a guest to sleep out in the freezing rain when there's shelter to be had."

"There's no rain today, lad," she said. "And ye'll find a place in the village, as I said before. If ye *are* the earl, they'll be glad to help ye." Her tone suggested that she didn't at all believe him. But as proof of her charity, she handed him a large hunk of bread. Iain tore off a piece, devouring the food, since he hadn't eaten in hours.

He wasn't going to give up on gaining a place to sleep. Not when he was convinced that he could prove himself by evening at the latest. All he needed to find was the signet ring that had been stolen.

When he'd finished the bread, he asked, "What of clothing, Mrs. Marlock?" He lowered his arms to his side, giving her a full view of his bare skin. "I can't be going around with naught to wear."

A faint blush rose over her cheeks and she sighed at last. "I suppose ye're right, at that. I'll see what rags we have, before ye gang to the village."

"I am grateful indeed. And thank you for the food." He inclined his head, and she eyed him as if not knowing what to do. In the end, she bobbed her own curtsy.

"Hattie!" she called out. One of the maids hurried inside the kitchen, a *cailín* of about sixteen. The girl sent him a curious look, and her gaze slid over his bare torso in open admiration. Though he rather felt like a roasted goose on display, Iain said nothing, in case the maid turned out to be an unexpected ally.

Mrs. Marlock said, "Stop yer gawpin, Hattie, and fetch the man some clothes."

The maid blushed and gave an embarrassed smile before hurrying away. Though Iain kept his expression masked, Mrs. Marlock moved in front of him and glared. "Once yer dressed, ye'll be leaving Penford. If ye *are* her ladyship's guest, ye'll get a full apology from me at that time." The look on her face said she doubted he would return.

"You'll see," he told her. "I will be dining at your table tonight." Once he had located his stolen belongings, he was confident that they would accept him.

Mrs. Marlock offered nothing more than an indignant "humph."

A few minutes later, Hattie brought him a ragged shirt and an equally tattered coat, along with a pair of shoes. Given the young girl's age and her attire that was slightly better than a kitchen maid's, he surmised she was a maid-of-all-work. And although he doubted if anything would fit, it was better than remaining half-naked and unshod. Iain thanked her for the clothes.

Unfortunately, it seemed he would be spending the next few hours out of doors, wearing servant's rags. A fine day this was turning out to be.

You never expected it to be easy, he reminded

himself. *Why should they believe you're an earl? Without any proof, how could they?*

He put on the ill-fitting shirt, coat, and shoes, taking the time he needed to make plans. Although he had hoped his men would join him here, it was beginning to seem that they had abandoned him. And with no servants to vouch for him, his circumstances had become dire indeed.

But he would never give up. Too many people were dependent on him.

After he was dressed, he followed Hattie down the servants' hallway. She turned to him and with a hopeful smile said, "I do wish you well, sir." Pointing to the door at the end, she added, "You can go out that way."

He eyed the door and then regarded the maid for a moment. "Do you believe that I am the Earl of Ashton, though I'm looking as if I'd been dragged through the midden heap?"

Hattie appeared uncomfortable and lowered her gaze. "It—it's not for me to be sayin', sir." With that, she continued leading him toward the back door.

He didn't argue with her, for she was only obeying orders. His mind was already conjuring up where he would stay this night. Possibly in the stables or somewhere sheltered. He hadn't a single coin to call his own, so no one in the village would give him a place.

Iain had only walked a few steps when he heard a woman screaming. The piercing noise made it sound as if she were being attacked. He didn't stop to ask questions, but hurried up the stairs leading to the hall. He found a middle-aged woman running toward the front door, her hair tangled and hanging down her back. She wore a long-sleeved blue serge gown and her eyes were wild. Far too young to be Lady Wolcroft, he guessed, but it could be the woman's daughter.

"Lady Penford!" Hattie exclaimed, rushing forward to her aid. "Please…let me help you."

Iain looked around to see what the woman was fleeing from, but there was nothing at all.

The woman's face was deathly white, and her hands shook badly. When Hattie put her hand out, Lady Penford gripped it hard. "Please, you have to help me! The—the wolves. I heard them howling. They're coming for me."

The maid sent a look toward Iain and shook her head in warning. Though Iain wasn't certain what was happening, it was clear that Lady Penford was suffering from visions that weren't real.

The woman started to bolt again, and Hattie tried to stop her, holding her by the waist. "My lady, no. You mustn't leave the house."

Whatever illness had captured her mind, Lady Penford might injure herself if she was allowed to flee. And though it wasn't his business, Iain stepped toward the doorway to keep her from escaping.

"Let me go," Lady Penford insisted, wrenching her way free of the maid. But when she moved toward the front door, Iain remained in place to block her. He sensed that this woman was trapped in a world of her own imaginings, one where reality made little sense.

"Where are the wolves?" he asked calmly. He kept his voice quiet, as though soothing a wounded animal.

His question seemed to break through Lady Penford's hysteria, and she faltered. "They—they were chasing me." Her face held confusion, and she appeared unaware that he was a stranger.

"Would you feel safer in your room?" he asked. "Perhaps Hattie could take you there."

"No." Her breathing grew unsteady. "I can't go back

there. The wolves will find me." She gripped her hands together and took another step toward the door. "Summon my coach."

He met Hattie's gaze, and she moved closer to Lady Penford. Iain took another step backward to prevent her from reaching the door.

A slight noise caught his attention at the top of the stairs, and he saw Lady Rose being carried by a footman. "Mother, please wait a moment." Her face paled at the sight of the matron, and she ordered, "Calvert, take me downstairs."

It sobered him to realize how difficult Lady Rose's life must be, having to rely on others to carry her where she wanted to go. The simple act of helping her mother would be quite beyond her abilities.

When she saw Iain standing by the door, her face tightened in dismay. Color flooded her cheeks as if she was embarrassed that he had witnessed her mother's outburst. Hattie brought a chair close to Lady Penford, and the footman set Lady Rose upon it, retreating to a discreet distance.

"Are you all right?" the young woman asked. In her voice, there was the gentle tone of compassion, no censure for the madness. She held out her hand, but Lady Penford ignored it.

At this close proximity, Iain noticed that Lady Rose's eyes were the color of warm sherry. A few tendrils of reddish-brown hair framed her lovely face, and he found himself wanting to ease her worry.

"Did you hear me, Mother?"

Lady Penford gave no answer, but she stared down at her trembling hands.

"I was just talking with Lady Penford about the wolves," Iain said, as if there were nothing at all wrong. He fixed his gaze upon the young woman, hoping she would play along, since the older woman seemed to be caught up in confusion.

But Lady Rose paid him no mind. "Everything is all right now, Mother. I am here." She reached out a hand, but the woman ignored it.

"I'm afraid," her mother admitted. Her eyes welled up with tears, and she twisted her hands together. "So afraid."

He glanced over at Lady Rose and saw her flushed cheeks. The maid and footman eyed one another before casting their gazes downward. Clearly the woman's madness was not a new occurrence.

"Is there anything I can do to help?" Iain asked.

The older woman turned back to him, and her mood suddenly shifted. "I've not seen you before. Do you know my son James? Is that why you are here? Has he returned from India?" Her voice was edged with emotion, and he suspected that grief and worry had led her into this agitated state.

Iain risked a glance toward Rose, who shook her head. It wasn't clear whether her brother was dead or gone, but he decided not to upset the woman any more than necessary. It was simple enough to continue with the ruse. "I might have seen him. Will you remind me of what he looks like?"

A sudden moment of clarity passed over the woman's face, and her expression filled up with sorrow. "James has been gone for a long time. I pray he will return, but he hasn't answered my letters. He must come back, you see. He is the new Earl of Penford." Her voice lowered to a soft whisper. "Now that my husband is…gone, there is so much to do. So many decisions to be made, and I can't—I simply can't—" Lady Penford covered her mouth with her hands, panic rising in her expression.

"You needn't worry," Rose reassured her. "Lily and I

will manage. Right now, I think you should go into the drawing room and have a cup of tea. Mrs. Marlock might have scones with clotted cream. Would you like that?"

The mention of food successfully diverted the matron's attention. "I—yes, that would be lovely."

"Hattie will take you to the drawing room, and we will join you there." Rose signaled for the maid to come forward, and Hattie guided Lady Penford down the hallway.

When her mother was gone, Rose turned back to Iain, and her expression held sadness. "Thank you for stopping her from leaving. She's been grieving ever since my father died."

He nodded. "She seemed very upset." *And not in her right mind,* he thought, but didn't say so. "Will she be all right?"

Rose sighed and straightened in the chair. "No one knows the answer to that question. There are good days and bad days."

He glanced back at the footman. "Do you need assistance? That is, if you wish to join her, I could—" But he stopped short, realizing how inappropriate it would be for him to carry her.

Lady Rose didn't appear to take offense, but simply answered, "Calvert will bring me there." Then she glanced at Iain's bedraggled clothing with a questioning look. "Do you still claim to be an Irish earl, sir?" Her words held a dry humor, and the look in her eyes said she didn't believe him at all.

Iain's mouth twisted in a smile. "My name is Lord Ashton, *a chara*. And you'll have to wait and see, won't you?"

CHAPTER TWO

Rose wasn't certain what to believe of this gentleman who claimed to be an earl. He lacked the deferential manners of a servant, especially after he'd taken charge of her mother's hysteria and calmed her. Even wearing rags, he *did* appear to be something more. But everything about him was improper, from his speech to his lack of formality. She simply couldn't believe that he was a nobleman—not without his own coach and servants.

Lord Ashton, was he? More like Lord of the Ashes.

Despite his appearance, he intrigued her. And yes, he *was* quite handsome, in a forbidden sort of way. The way he'd smiled at her was both wicked and filled with promises of dark corners and secret liaisons. His dark hair needed to be trimmed, and his cheeks held the stubble of a beard, making her wonder what it would be like to touch it.

Her mind was wandering as badly as her mother's. Why was he truly here? And who was he?

Calvert brought her into the drawing room to join her mother. Her sister, Lily, arrived shortly afterward. Rose met her sister's questioning look, and she shook her head slightly to let her know that this was not a good day. *Tread softly, Lily.*

"Mother, would you like tea?" her sister asked brightly, reaching for the silver teapot.

Iris's face had gone distant, and Lily had to repeat herself twice more before their mother blinked and turned to face them. "What was that? Oh, yes, tea. With milk and sugar, if you please."

Lily prepared the tea and sat beside their mother as she offered her the cup. Iris did appear calmer, but neither of them wanted to say anything to bring back the fearful visions.

"Are you feeling well today, Mother?" Lily poured another cup for Rose and set it before her.

"Yes, I am much better now. But who was that new gentleman I saw a moment ago?"

Dash it all, she'd hoped her mother would forget all about Lord of the Ashes. Her sister sent her a curious look, for she had not seen the stranger who had arrived at Penford. Rose decided it was best to say nothing.

"He's no one, Mother. You needn't worry." She didn't want her mother distracted or afraid of a stranger.

"A new gentleman?" Lily prompted.

Don't, Rose warned her silently, raising an eyebrow. Now was not the time to discuss it.

But Iris turned and sent her a mysterious smile. "He *was* rather dashing. I'm not blind, my dear. Was he here to pay a call on you?" Before she could tell her mother no and attempt to change the subject, Lady Penford continued, "You *are* in need of a husband, after all, Rose."

An unbidden rush of embarrassment gathered inside her, and Lily interrupted them. "Not now, Mother. It's too soon." Her sister distracted Iris with a sugar biscuit, redirecting their conversation to a new gown she planned to have made. *Thank you, Lily.*

But even so, it hurt that her mother would say something so thoughtless when Rose already had a suitor. Her eyes welled up with tears, and she blinked hard to hold them back.

I will not cry. But the very thought of Lord Burkham made her emotional, for she missed him so much. He had been on the verge of offering for her when she had fallen ill in Yorkshire. The terrible sickness had forced her to battle for her life, and when it was over, she was left too weak to move. Thomas had sent letters over the past few months, wishing her well. She was confident that when she could walk again, he would ask her to marry him.

Rose refused to surrender to a life where she had to be carried like a child. No matter how long it took, she would not return to London until she could walk. Perhaps it was her pride, but she didn't want Thomas to see her as an invalid.

"You really ought to return to London for the Season," Iris continued. "You are such a lovely young woman. Any gentleman would be glad to marry someone as sweet as you."

Rose tried to muster a smile, but it felt as if a weight were crushing her chest. Iris seemed to have forgotten all about her inability to walk. "I cannot return for a few more months. But Lily might wish to go."

"No, I—I would rather not attend the Season," Lily stammered. Her sister sat down and chose a large tea cake, stuffing it into her mouth to avoid further conversation. Then she gathered two more and piled them upon her plate, making it clear that she would continue eating so she would not have to speak. Rose raised an eyebrow at the pile of food, but Lily sent her a pained smile. Both of them were in the same dilemma, truthfully. They had already selected their future husbands; it was simply that fate had intervened.

Lily had been avoiding marriage ever since Matthew Larkspur, the Earl of Arnsbury, had gone missing. Rose was certain she was waiting for the gentleman to return...if he ever did. Her sister pined for Lord Arnsbury, and she seemed eager to shut herself away from society to avoid choosing someone else.

Iris sipped at her tea, and she suddenly sent Rose a gentle smile. "It will be all right, my darlings. Both you and your sister will one day marry the men of your dreams. I believe that."

In that moment, their mother no longer appeared to be the same woman who was fleeing from imaginary wolves. Instead, the moment of clarity revealed a woman who was once again trying to find happiness for her daughters.

Rose searched in desperation for another topic of conversation. "Do you suppose it will rain today?"

"Now, do not try to change the subject," Iris chided. "You are my eldest daughter, and it's high time you were wed. How old are you now? Twenty?"

"Twenty-three," she murmured.

Her mother frowned. "No, that's not possible." As she began trying to convince her that she was only twenty, Rose pasted a smile on her face and let her thoughts drift. She didn't want to think about the undeniable fact that she was likely to remain a spinster unless she learned to walk again.

She hadn't given up—not at all. Every day she practiced standing, and though her legs would not yet support her weight, she refused to abandon hope. She had to rebuild her strength, and if force of will would move her legs, then she would indeed walk again.

"It is unlikely, but not impossible," the doctor had

said. And Rose had held fast to that fragment of hope, needing to believe it.

Outside, she saw movement, and when she focused her gaze, she realized it was the Irishman, Mr. Donovan. It appeared that he was walking toward the stables.

Now what was he doing? Her curiosity was piqued, and more than anything, she wanted to follow him.

But being unable to walk meant that she was never alone. She could go nowhere without help, and she didn't exactly want the footman to think she was infatuated with the man-who-claimed-to-be-an-earl. No, she was merely intrigued by his story—that was all.

"Rose, what is your opinion?" Lily interrupted her thoughts, and she jerked her attention back to them.

"I—that is, whatever you think would be best."

"Excellent." Iris beamed at her. "This will be most splendid."

Now what exactly had she agreed to? When she risked a glimpse at Lily, her sister was wincing and shaking her head. Oh dear.

Rose cleared her throat, waiting for her mother to elaborate. Iris finished her tea, looking entirely too satisfied. "Very well, then. Both of you will go to London as soon as your grandmother returns. And by the end of the summer, I shall expect one or both of you to have a husband."

London? No, not that. She'd rather be devoured by the aforementioned wolves.

Iris rose to her feet and was already talking about the details of the upcoming Season. "I shall speak with Mrs. Marlock about ordering new gowns for both of you. And then… I won't have to worry so much." Her voice trailed away softly as she reached the doorway.

The moment their mother was gone, Lily let out a groan. "London? Rose, what were you thinking?"

"I wasn't listening," she confessed. "I was distracted."

"Obviously." Her sister stood and began pacing. "We have to convince her that she only imagined it. We are not going to London to be married off. Especially me."

"Because of Lord Arnsbury?" she ventured.

Lily's face flushed, and there was a flash of grief. "He might come back. And if he does..." There were years of hope bound up in that wish, for her sister loved the earl with all her being. But it had been nearly two years since he'd disappeared. The chances of him returning were growing slimmer each day, and she didn't ask what Lily would do if he never came back.

"Whether or not he does, we have a problem." Rose used both of her arms to press hard against the chair, attempting to stand again. "Lily, help me up."

Her sister came to support her waist, and in her expression, Rose saw sympathy. "Are you certain you can stand?"

"My arms are getting stronger." She *would* manage somehow.

But her sister took a step back. "Oughtn't you to ask Calvert? He's stronger than I and could help if you stumbled."

With reluctance, Rose lowered herself back down. "No. Never mind." Though she understood that Lily didn't believe she could stand, it dimmed her spirits. Her throat tightened, and she took a deep breath. "What should we do about Mother?"

"I think we should behave as if she never brought it up. Pretend she never suggested any of it. Like the wolves. She won't remember in the morning."

"I suppose so." Rose risked a glance out the window again, and it bothered her that she had lost sight of Mr. Donovan. Where was he now? She craned her neck, but still could not see him.

"*What* is it that has you so distracted, Rose?" Lily peered outside the window and then turned back. "It's him, isn't it? The gentleman you spoke of."

She sighed. "Well, yes. Mr. Donovan claims he's an earl, but I don't believe him."

Lily wrinkled her nose. "An earl? Why would he say such a thing?"

"I have no idea. But I wonder why he's truly here." The logical explanation was that he was attempting to insinuate himself within their household for a nefarious purpose. And yet…she didn't quite believe that.

Her sister's knuckles tightened on the window, and she shook her head. "Oh no."

"What?" Rose couldn't see anything from her vantage point.

"It seems that you were right about Mr. Donovan. I don't think he's an earl at all."

It was maddening being unable to see, and Rose used all her strength to hoist her weight against the arms of the chair. "Why would you say that, Lily?"

Lily turned back with an apologetic look. "Because he's stealing one of our horses."

Iain urged the gelding into a hard gallop, guiding the horse toward the spot where he'd been robbed. Behind him, he heard the sounds of men yelling, "Stop, thief!"

Which was ironic, really, because this was *his* horse, even if no one here would believe him. He'd been shocked to find Darcy inside the stables, where he'd been intending to conceal himself for the night. Someone had put the gelding in one of the stalls, and that meant the boys were nearby. This time, Iain intended to confront them and seize the rest of his missing belongings.

More than all else, he needed that signet ring. Or at the very least, the letter from Lady Wolcroft inviting him to Penford.

He was convinced that the robbery was adolescent mischief. They had somehow knocked him from his horse—possibly with a rope strung between the trees—and had entertained themselves by stripping him of everything.

Iain, however, was not amused. Their trickery had cost him his identity, and he would hunt them down until he had everything back.

He leaned in, searching his surroundings for a sign of the boys. The afternoon sun was blinding, but he found the lake easily enough. The road grew narrower, and at last, he spied one of the boys walking alone. He looked to be about thirteen or so and was wearing Iain's coat. The moment he heard Iain coming up behind him, he broke into a run.

Not fast enough.

Iain leaned down and seized the boy, dragging him atop his horse. The lad was skinny, and though he fought, Iain gripped him hard. "You're not going anywhere. Not until you've returned everything you stole from me."

"I didn't steal anything. I was bringing it back," the boy complained.

"Like the clothes you're wearing? And what did you do with my signet ring?" Iain had no sympathy for him. The lad had questions he was going to answer. "I'm thinking we should speak to your father about this."

The boy sent him a sly smile. "He's not at home." The gleeful expression on his face made it obvious that he *wanted* Iain to take him home.

Perhaps it was better to take a different tack. "Then you'll be coming with me. Unless you want to return my ring first?"

He didn't truly know *what* he would do with the boy, but he wasn't about to let the lad go free. Not until he had answers.

"I don't have it." To prove his point, the boy showed his empty hands.

"Then where is it?" he demanded. The boy's answer was a shrug. His expression remained defiant, as if he intended to hold his silence.

Iain reached inside the coat pockets, and not only was the ring missing, but also the letter from Lady Wolcroft. Damn it all, that was the proof he needed. And the smug expression on the lad's face only irritated him.

Continuing this line of questioning would lead him nowhere. It was unlikely the boy would tell him anything. Iain decided to try a different tactic. He gripped the boy in the saddle and turned Darcy back toward Penford. The servants there might know who he was and what to do with him. Iain could also summon the boy's father if need be.

As they rode onward, the lad remarked, "Are you kidnapping me?" The hopeful tone made it sound as if he was eager to be abducted.

He decided not to answer the question, since it was clear that the boy was unafraid of anything. Threats would do no good whatsoever, and until Iain found out what the boy valued, he would get none of his possessions returned. He continued riding toward Penford and asked, "Why did you and your companion steal my belongings?"

"I didn't steal anything. The horse followed me, so I decided to take him to Penford. It's probably where he came from."

Iain didn't believe that for a moment. "And what about my clothing? You just happened to find it and take it from me?"

"I *did* find it. It was on the ground near the stream where I found the horse."

The boy's story was filled with holes. Someone had knocked him from his horse and robbed him. And he just "happened" to find Iain's horse and coat? No, not a word of his story was true.

"You're lying, lad."

The boy lowered his shoulders and gave a dramatic sigh. Rolling his eyes, he said, "You're right, of course. I dragged you from your horse, and then I stole it and your clothing to trade for food for my family."

"At least your second story is more believable. Aside from needing food." Iain turned the boy's palm over. This was a lad who had hardly worked a day in his life. His fingernails were neatly pared and no dirt was beneath them. Not to mention his speech held the air of nobility. "You've never gone hungry in your life."

"And how would *you* know?"

The boy's taunt awakened the dark memories without warning. Iain had seen far more hunger than he'd ever dreamed of—and those nightmares would be with him always. Too many of his friends had weakened and died. Though Ashton had not suffered as much as other areas, the lack of food had devastated the tenants. Iain would never forget the cries of the children, or the wailing of their mothers when an infant succumbed to starvation.

"Because I have seen people die from hunger. And you're nowhere close to that."

The boy seemed to sense the shift in his mood and said nothing. He also stopped struggling on the horse.

"What is your name?" Iain asked. "And you'd best be

telling me the truth because Lady Penford's servants will know who you are, won't they?"

The boy hesitated, but admitted, "My name is Beau." The lad didn't offer anything further, but Iain was convinced that he was a nobleman's son. Everything from the boy's speech, to his disdain for authority, spoke of breeding.

In the countryside, everyone knew everyone. If he caused a stir or demanded justice, they likely would defend their own, for *he* was the outsider here. But the lad appeared to have little respect for consequences, and it was likely that he had played tricks of this nature before.

It took only moments to reach the estate, where he found the coachman waiting for him. The man's face was purple with fury, and other servants had gathered around.

"What the devil is going on?" the coachman demanded. "First ye go off with one of our—" He paused a moment and inspected the gelding. His expression transformed and some of his anger faded. "This isn't one of our horses."

"No. He's *my* horse, Darcy," Iain said. "And I'll be taking him back to the stables now." He dismounted and pulled Beau off the horse, still gripping him by the arm. "This lad stole him from me, along with my clothes."

With that, he stripped the boy of the coat. The fabric was torn near the hem, and it was filthy. He glared at Beau, folding the coat under his arm. "He and his friend thought it would be a lark to steal." An idea sparked suddenly, one that perfectly fit the boy's crime. "And since he stole my horse, I believe he'll be spending the afternoon mucking out your stables as punishment."

The coachman looked uneasy about the prospect.

"Well, I don't rightly know. Is this true, Master Beauregard?"

The boy lifted his chin. "I didn't steal anything. I found them."

"I'm certain your parents would be wanting to know of your mischief," Iain remarked. "You and your friend."

"As I've said before, my father isn't here." His tone held a note of triumph, as if no one could hold him accountable.

"Sir Lester should return within a day or two," the coachman remarked.

Iain realized he'd been right about the boy's family. Beau was either the son of a knight or a baronet.

Yet at the mention of his father, the boy grew defensive. "He wouldn't believe any of you. And if I find out anyone has told him, every last one of you will be dismissed." He stiffened and shot a glare at all of them, fixing his final stare upon Iain.

"I cannot be dismissed," Iain said to the coachman. "Can I?"

The older man's mouth twitched. It was clear that he found the boy's threat irritating. "Nay, you cannot." Especially since Iain was not employed by the household.

Before the coachman could say anything further, Iain said, "Then there is no problem with him spending the afternoon shoveling horse droppings, as punishment, is there? I will take it upon myself to see that he does a fine job of it." Without waiting for a reply, he guided the boy back toward the stables. He caught a glimpse of amusement from the servants, and not one of them voiced their protest. Like as not, this was a rare chance for the boy to face consequences.

As he glanced behind him one last time, he saw a

face pressed up to a window of the house. It was Lady Rose, watching them. Iain sent her a smile and bowed slightly, before he escorted the boy into the stables.

It was nearly sunset when Rose finally got up the nerve to visit the stables. Calvert wasn't at all happy about it, but he had no choice in the matter. "It's too dark to be riding, Lady Rose. I can take you in the morning, if you like."

But she wasn't here to ride. She had waited for Mr. Donovan to leave the stables, fully expecting him to be on his way. Yet hours had passed, and no one seemed surprised that he was still here. It was as if he'd bewitched the servants into believing his tale.

All she knew was that he'd returned with the horse. It seemed that it had been a misunderstanding of some kind, and somehow Sir Lester's son, Beauregard, had been involved.

"I want to know why Mr. Donovan is still here," she said. Calvert shrugged. Her footman had never been much for conversation, and at the moment, it frustrated her to no end. "Well?"

"He's supervising whilst the boy mucks out the stables, so I've heard."

"Why on earth would they be doing that? I thought he'd left hours ago."

The footman seemed at a loss for words. When he couldn't gather up an explanation, Rose waved her hand in dismissal. "Just take me to the stables, and I'll find out for myself."

The footman grumbled about her orders, but he reluctantly obeyed. He carried her through the gardens, and as he walked, Rose tried to think of what to say to

Mr. Donovan. She should ask him to leave again, but curiosity was overruling her common sense. Well, that, and the fact that the man was the most handsome servant she'd ever seen.

When they reached the stables at last, the door was ajar. The strong odor of horse manure assaulted her nostrils, and she found Donovan standing beside Beauregard. The young boy wore a furious expression, and he was covered in filth. Perspiration had dampened his shirt, and he shoveled another pile of manure while the Irishman watched.

"Nearly finished, lad. You've paid the price for your folly, I'd say. If you're wanting to tell me where my ring is, you can stop."

Beau didn't respond to the comment, but instead continued shoveling. It was the first time she'd ever seen him engaged in any kind of labor. His face was thunderous, but he had filled a wheelbarrow with droppings. The coachman, Nelson, was busy trimming one of the horse's hooves near the far end of the stable.

Mr. Donovan turned when he heard them enter. "Lady Rose, it's glad I am to see you once again. Although I'm not so very presentable at the moment." He sent her a rueful grin. She noticed, then, that he was wearing a different coat. It was still dirty and a bit worn, but it *did* have more of the look of a nobleman than the rags he'd worn earlier.

"Why is Beauregard working in the stables?" she asked. And why was the Irishman overseeing the boy's efforts? It wasn't his place to do so if he had been ordered to leave the estate.

"This young lad robbed me of my horse and belongings when I arrived here," Mr. Donovan explained. "He agreed to muck out the stables as punishment for his mischief. And in the morning, he will bring back everything that belongs to me. That is, unless he wishes to clean the stables again."

Rose doubted if Beauregard had "agreed" to anything. But strangely, he *had* completed the task. She studied his face, but the boy refused to meet her gaze. Instead, he shoveled another heap of dung, ignoring both of them.

"Where is your father, Beauregard?" she asked the boy.

At that, he turned, and shot her a glare. "He was supposed to return three days ago."

Mr. Donovan caught her gaze, and Rose understood his silent nod. She had the feeling that he had also promised not to tell Sir Lester of his son's misdeeds. For a moment, his green eyes lingered upon hers, and she could almost sense his thoughts: *The boy needs his father.*

They all knew it. Beauregard constantly caused trouble, due to his father's lengthy absences. Most of the folk were thankful when he returned to school after the holidays. Which made her wonder why Beau was here, instead of at Eton. She didn't voice her suspicions, but instead remarked, "Won't your family be looking for you, Beau?"

"There's naught to be worried about," Mr. Donovan said. "I sent word to his household that he was paying a call upon you and your sisters and would be back at nightfall."

Beauregard shot him a sullen look, and rested his shovel against the stall. "My father *will* be angry at you for this when he returns. I told you, I wasn't the one who stole from you." He grumbled beneath his breath, muttering something about a horse that had followed him.

Mr. Donovan ignored the threat and added, "You

missed a spot in the corner, lad. Finish it, and then we'll bring you home. After you've washed up, that is."

"We?" Rose asked.

"Aye, *a chara.* You can accompany us when I take the lad home again. Then we'll talk, and you can ask me all the questions you're wanting to." He strode over to the end of the stables and brought out Molly, one of the older mares. "Bring Calvert as a chaperone, if you'd like."

"That would be *Mister* Calvert to you," the footman corrected with a glare. Iain only ignored the man.

But the coachman stepped away from the horse he was tending and intervened. "Lady Rose needn't go anywhere," Nelson argued. "Especially with the likes of you."

At the sight of the mare, Lady Rose hesitated. "I don't know. I haven't been riding in some time, and—" Her words broke away. From the look on her footman's face, she could tell that he had no desire to go anywhere. Nelson also seemed unwilling to condone it.

But then, it was her decision, was it not?

"It's not so very far, is it, lad?" Though Mr. Donovan directed the words to Beauregard, he never took his gaze from hers. His green eyes held interest, and she felt a prickle of awareness toward the man. His shirt was damp with perspiration, and it outlined rigid muscles. She wondered exactly how strong he was, and a blush stole over her face. Even Lord Burkham had never looked at her in such a way...as if he were trying to know her intimately. The thought unnerved her.

"It's about three miles," Rose heard herself answer. Her brain argued that she had no business escorting Beauregard home—not with this man. He was an Irish stranger whose flirtatious demeanor was entirely improper.

And yet, she'd felt so trapped in the past few weeks,

any outing was a welcome opportunity—even if it was only for a chance to leave the estate. She was so weary of being inside, unable to move or go anywhere without the curmudgeonly Calvert.

"Three miles isn't a long journey at all. And it is a fine evening, to be sure." Mr. Donovan reached for one of the saddles and began readying Molly.

Nelson started to protest, but Lady Rose lifted a hand and shook her head at the coachman. It was not his place to deny her the right to ride.

Once Mr. Donovan had cinched the saddle, he beckoned to her. "Bring Lady Rose here," he told the footman, "and you can return to the house if you've no wish to go with her."

"I won't be leaving her with the likes of you," Calvert countered. And while Rose could understand his reasoning, the idea of a ride tempted her. It *was* a lovely evening, and despite her inner doubts, was there any harm in riding a few miles down the road? She didn't think so.

"Put me upon Molly," she ordered her footman. "I'll be fine."

"But, Lady Rose, you cannot consider this." Calvert appeared aghast at the idea. "You don't even know this man."

"No," she agreed. But she did want to know more about him and why he had come to Penford. It would give her the chance to ascertain whether he was telling the truth. "You are welcome to follow on your own mount, if you wish. Or Nelson can accompany me." The coachman looked uncomfortable at the idea.

Calvert also appeared uneasy. "I can't be leaving you alone with the Irishman."

"Then come with me." She pointed toward the mare. "But help me onto Molly first."

He brought her over to the horse, looking uneasy about her decision. Rose sent him a pointed look, reminding Calvert that he was in her employ. Eventually, he lifted her onto the mare. She sat sidesaddle and guided the animal to the door. "Thank you. I shall wait outside until you decide whether to attend me yourself or send another servant."

The footman sent her a weary look, but nodded. "I know my duty, Lady Rose." With the greatest of reluctance, he went to fetch his own horse with the help of Nelson.

Mr. Donovan clapped his arm on Beauregard and followed. "Come, lad. We'll get you washed up before you go home."

Resentment was written all over the boy's face, but he obeyed. Rose guided the mare out of the stables and toward the path. A moment later, Mr. Donovan led the adolescent boy from the stable toward the water trough, and ordered the boy to strip off his shirt.

Beau looked disgruntled, but did as he was told, washing his face, arms, and torso. Donovan did the same, splashing water on his face and throat. Droplets of water spilled over his skin, while his hair was wet along his forehead and cheeks. He turned to her, as if he'd sensed her watching, and he sent her the pirate smile again.

Rose felt her cheeks warm, unsure of why she was so intrigued by this man. There was a sense of rebellion about him, as if he obeyed no rules but his own. But she felt her own mouth respond with an answering smile.

He's dangerous, she thought to herself. Her skin tightened, as if by an invisible caress. She followed the trail of a water droplet as it slid down his throat to his chest. Never before had she been so entranced by a man. It was better to avert her gaze, to prevent herself from imagining such wickedness.

She didn't understand her own reaction, for she should not be looking at Iain Donovan. He was a visitor, nothing more. Her heart belonged to Thomas, and this was nothing but idle foolishness.

The mare started to graze as she waited. Beauregard finished washing, while the Irishman helped Calvert saddle up their horses.

When Mr. Donovan returned, he was riding the black gelding he'd taken earlier, while Nelson led a second horse outside. The coachman helped Beauregard mount the animal, while Calvert followed on his own horse. Then Mr. Donovan drew his gelding beside her mare. Although their horses were of similar size, he was still far taller than she.

"This is Darcy," he told her. She leaned over to touch the horse, and the gelding snorted.

"He's beautiful."

"He's friendly enough. But I can't say as he's the most intelligent horse I've ever had." He sent her a conspiratorial smile. "Frightened of everything, he is."

"Then why did you choose him?" Most men would take a spirited stallion instead of this one.

"Because no one else wanted him." He gave the horse's jaw a friendly pat. "He may not have the wits of a field mouse, but he's a good sort, is Darcy." With that, he gestured for her to move forward. "Lead on, Lady Rose."

She did, and oh, it felt wonderful to be ambulatory, even if it was only on horseback. Rose breathed in the evening air, sighing with thankfulness. For a moment, she pretended that her legs were whole, that she was not dependent upon others. She held fast to the dream, knowing that it would end as soon as Calvert helped her dismount.

But for now, it was enough.

She wanted to urge the horse faster, to feel the wind against her hair. That would only end the ride sooner, so she refrained. Instead, she drank in the sight of her surroundings, enjoying the sunlight as the last of the day disappeared. The dirt road meandered over hills and by the river, and she felt the breath of spring upon her face.

"You look as if you're starving to be outside," Mr. Donovan said. "How long has it been?"

She stiffened in the saddle. "I sit in the garden every day."

"How long has it been since you've left the estate?" he corrected.

"Since we arrived in early December." They had only a few neighbors who dwelled in the country, and when her mother's mental state had worsened, it had seemed prudent to bring her here, where it was private.

When Mr. Donovan looked as if he wanted to ply her with more questions, Rose patted the horse and urged the mare into a trot. He countered by bringing his horse alongside hers. "Are you afraid of me, Lady Rose?"

"Now why should I be afraid of a groom?" she countered. "That is who you are, am I right? You seem to know your way around a stable."

"You know that's not who I am." He kept his pace even with hers and sent her a dark smile. "I told you. I am the Earl of Ashton, and your grandmother invited me here."

She still didn't believe that. There were too many flaws in his story, most notably, the absence of servants. A peer would never arrive at an estate on horseback. And although he claimed that there was a coach accident and that he'd left his servants behind, she could never imagine an earl doing such a thing. For one, it was dangerous. For another, it made no sense at all.

"My grandmother isn't here," she reminded him. "Why would she invite you to come if she was on holiday in Bath?"

"She told me I was welcome to visit your family anytime this year. I sent word, but apparently my letter didn't arrive."

She glanced at him again, wondering if he might be telling the truth. Letters were frequently missed, so it was indeed conceivable. But she couldn't bring herself to trust him. At least, not yet.

"My grandmother is not a fool. If she does not believe your tale of being the Earl of Ashton, she'll toss you out on your ear."

"As you would like to do?" He shrugged. "You'll see, Lady Rose. She *has* met me, and your mother and mine were friends."

Highly unlikely. "Then why have I never heard of you?"

His expression grew shielded. "I've never been to England before, unlike my older brother."

She didn't miss the hint of pain when he mentioned a brother, but she didn't inquire about the family death. Yet his claim, that he had never visited England, struck her as preposterous. A younger son would have to visit London from time to time.

"So your family neglected you in your training to become the earl."

His hands tightened upon the reins of his horse. "That was their choice, not mine. And I intend to remedy that immediately." He glanced behind him at Beauregard. "This lad stole my brother's signet ring. So *he* knows I am the earl."

The boy let out an exasperated huff of air. "I never saw a ring. He probably *is* a groom. And I'll tell Father how he forced me to shovel dung. If you hadn't come when you did, he might have forced me to eat it."

The boy's resentful words were spoken as if he wanted Rose to be aghast at his misfortune. Mr. Donovan only laughed at the boy and said, "Hardly. But if you don't bring back everything in the morning, I might consider it."

He winked at Rose, and the harmless teasing unnerved her in a way she didn't understand. Even if, God help her, he *was* an earl, he would never spend this much time flirting with a woman like her.

Unless he desired her fortune.

Yes, that was undoubtedly the reason. He hardly knew her at all, and she couldn't even walk. She decided to ignore his flirting, for it meant nothing.

They continued riding down the dirt road, and she grew quiet, savoring the evening light. The sky was transforming from a soft blue into a darker indigo. Upon the horizon, the setting sun gleamed its golden rays.

Beauregard looked as if he wanted to ride on ahead of them, but Mr. Donovan kept him close, holding the reins of his horse.

"I can go home on my own," the young man asserted. "I know the way."

"Children should be seen and not heard," was Iain Donovan's answer. Rose had to hide her smile at Beauregard's indignant glare.

"I'm not a child."

"Aye, you are. Only a child bent on mischief would be stealing a man's shirt and coat. Unless you believe yourself to be a man, in which case I'd have to bring you to the authorities for a more appropriate punishment."

Rose glanced back at Iain, wondering if he truly meant it. But she spied the amusement in his eyes.

"Go and ride alongside Calvert," he bade the young

man. "But don't try to flee home without us, else I *will* drag you back."

For a fleeting moment, Beauregard looked uncertain of whether to accept the freedom. But he took advantage of the offer, guiding his mount back to ride alongside the footman. It gave Rose and Iain a slight measure of privacy to their conversation.

"Calvert, if the lad attempts to ride home on his own, bring him back to me," the Irishman ordered. The footman only shook his head and muttered.

"He's not very cooperative, is he?" Mr. Donovan said. "What about you, Lady Rose? If the boy attempts to flee, will you help me hunt him down?"

She started to argue, but then realized it was all in fun. With a serious nod, she said, "I shall send my mother's wolves after him."

A wide, appreciative smile slid over his face. "A fine idea, to be sure."

Though there was an easy tone to his voice, offering friendship, his eyes were watching her with interest. Her cheeks warmed, and she tried to pay it no mind. To shift his attention, she asked, "Where do you live in Ireland, Mr. Donovan?"

"In the west, not far from Connemara. There are mountains there, and green meadows so beautiful, they would break your heart." His expression held love, but there was also a trace of tension in his tone.

"I've heard stories about the famine," she said. "So many have left. Is it as bad as they say?"

His face grew somber, and his eyes remained fixed upon the road. An invisible shadow seemed to pass over him, and his tone darkened. "Worse than anyone could ever imagine."

"I'm sorry." She had heard about the hundreds of thousands of men and women leaving their homes. The workhouses were filled with the poor, and many Irish had sought work in textile mills and factories. Even then, there were not enough positions.

"There's hardly any food left in Ireland," he continued. "No one has money to buy anything. My mother and sisters went to New York to stay with family, while I came here."

"Will you join them there?"

He shook his head. "I made a promise to take care of the tenants at Ashton. I must return to them by the end of summer."

So he still maintained he was an earl. While it was indeed possible that he could possess a title, she didn't quite believe him. Instead, she kept the conversation centered on what she knew to be true. "Did you lose your crops?"

He fixed his gaze upon the road, expression grim. "The blight struck us hard, and a great deal of the land is wasted now. But we will bring back supplies and replant the fields."

"*We*?" Was there someone else who had come with him?

"My wife and I." He cast his gaze upon her again, and this time, *she* was the one who was surprised. Perhaps she'd been mistaken in thinking he had come to England in search of a wife.

"So...you're already married, then?" The thought seemed impossible, especially given the way he had been staring at her.

"Not yet. But if you're offering, *a chara,* I'd be glad to accept." He sent her a teasing smile, and it seemed that his mood had shifted from the earlier melancholy.

She sent him a wry look. "I was hardly proposing marriage, Mr. Donovan." She wasn't so desperate as that. "Besides, I already have a gentleman suitor."

"Have you?" His face brightened. "I cannot say I'm surprised to hear it. Any man would be honored to wed a *cailín* as fair as you."

Although his words were kind, she wasn't interested in idle flirting. "Yes, well. You can turn your interests somewhere else."

"Is he here, then? Your betrothed husband?"

"No, he's in London."

"I can't believe that's wise. Leaving a beautiful woman such as yourself at the mercy of the local swains. You might change your mind about marrying him."

She didn't bother to correct him, that Lord Burkham had not yet asked for her hand in marriage. It might be true enough one day soon. She wasn't going to fall prey to meaningless compliments when there were far more serious matters at hand.

"So you intend to find a bride with the help of my grandmother, is that it?" She wondered what sort of woman he hoped to woo. It wasn't going to be easy, for few women would marry a man who wanted her for nothing but money. Only someone quite desperate. Ireland lay in ruins, and it was unlikely that any woman would want to live there.

"Indeed. Unless you change your mind, that is." He reached out and took her gloved hand. His touch lingered upon her, warming the kidskin glove. When he stared into her eyes, she had a sudden rash thought that he was about to kiss her. Right here, in front of her footman and Beauregard.

"Keep your hands to yourself, Mr. Donovan. Or I shall be forced to whack you with a parasol."

"Or a rake," he suggested cheerfully. He winked at her, and she relaxed when she realized that he was only teasing her.

"I could be quite lethal with gardening tools. You don't

want to imagine what I would do with a pair of shears."

He winced and made a face. "You terrify me."

Her smile widened. "You *should* be scared. I can be quite fierce when provoked."

"I can easily believe that." His green eyes locked upon hers. "You are a strong woman, Lady Rose. You would tell everyone to go and kiss the devil's backside before you'd turn away from your family or those who need you. Am I wrong?"

Rose blinked a moment at his assumption. No, he wasn't wrong that she would fight to the death to protect her loved ones. "It's true that I will always stand by my family." She straightened in the saddle and regarded him. Though she didn't know why she was telling him this, she felt the need to insist, "But more than that, I also intend to walk again."

He studied her for a moment as if he wanted to ask questions. But he simply gave a nod of acceptance. "You will."

His quiet confidence should have reassured her. But instead, she found herself confessing to him, "I am well aware that no man wishes to marry a woman who cannot walk. I've been trying for months, but no matter how hard I try, I fall. Every time. I just...don't know how long it will take for me to rebuild my strength."

"All you can do is get up and try again," he said. "If you want something badly enough, you won't give up."

She turned to look at him, and when she met his gaze, she saw a challenge there. "You're right. I suppose I have to keep trying—no matter how long it takes."

If you enjoyed the excerpt, you may purchase it at: www.michellewillingham.com/book/good-earls-dont-lie.

Kindle bestselling author and Rita® Award finalist **Michelle Willingham** has published more than thirty-five romance novels and novellas. Currently, she lives in southeastern Virginia with her husband and children, and is working on more historical romance books in a variety of settings, such as medieval and Viking-era Ireland, medieval Scotland, and Victorian and Regency England. When she's not writing, Michelle enjoys baking, playing the piano, and avoiding exercise at all costs. Her books have been translated into languages around the world and are also available in audio. Visit her website at www.michellewillingham.com to find English and foreign translations.